'Oh, for heaven

Beth's patience bro
bore. 'Look, there n
why you're here. As
to do your job I don
find life a bit easier for all of us if you're at
least prepared to be civil.'

'I'm quite prepared to be civil, Dr Sanderson,'
Ewan said coldly.

'Just not friendly.'

'That's right.'

Dear Reader

We travel the world this month, and introduce a new author to our list in Rebecca Lang, whose MIDNIGHT SUN takes us to the far north of Canada. We think you'll like her! Margaret Barker is back with THE DOCTOR'S DAUGHTER, a rewarding change of pace and style. Then to Australia for Judith Ansell's HEARTS OUT OF TIME, and Marion Lennox's ONE CARING HEART, both tear-jerkers you will love! Excellent holiday reading.

The Editor

!!!STOP PRESS!!! If you enjoy reading these medical books, have you ever thought of writing one? We are always looking for new writers for LOVE ON CALL, and want to hear from you. Send for the guidelines, and start writing!

Marion Lennox has had a variety of careers — medical receptionist, computer programmer and teacher. Married, with two young children, she now lives in rural Victoria, Australia. Her wish for an occupation which would allow her to remain at home with her children, her dog and the budgie led her to attempt writing a novel.

Recent titles by the same author:

LEGACY OF SHADOWS
A LOVING LEGACY
THE LAST EDEN

ONE CARING HEART

BY

MARION LENNOX

MILLS & BOON LIMITED
ETON HOUSE, 18–24 PARADISE ROAD
RICHMOND, SURREY, TW9 1SR

MILLS & BOON, the Rose Device and LOVE ON CALL are trademarks of the publisher.

First published in Great Britain 1994
by Mills & Boon Limited

© Marion Lennox 1994

Australian copyright 1994   Philippine copyright 1994
This edition 1994

ISBN 0 263 78708 7

Set in 10 on 11½ pt Linotron Times
03-9407-56286

Typeset in Great Britain by Centracet, Cambridge
Made and printed in Great Britain

CHAPTER ONE

IN HER next life, Dr Beth Sanderson didn't intend being a doctor! Beth thought longingly of different careers as she locked her surgery door — of jobs with regular tea-breaks and weekends off and lunch-hours! 'Especially with lunch-hours,' she muttered to herself, acknowledging the hollow feeling in the pit of her stomach. Beth had missed lunch. She was late for her dinner and now. . . Now Micky Edgar was crouched on her back path, cradling his dog.

'Dr Beth, Buster's hurt his pad.' Micky looked up at the young woman doctor as he spoke, his eyes trusting. Despite initial reservations about a lady doctor, the islanders had quickly taken this softly spoken, green-eyed girl to their hearts and Micky was no exception.

Although Beth was twenty-seven years old and Micky Edgar was not quite twelve, Micky privately thought Dr Beth was just the sort of lady he could marry. He loved her bouncy, shoulder-length brown curls, her wide, welcoming smile and the way she had of laughing with a soft, gurgly chuckle at things most grown-ups didn't even think were funny. Still, marriage was the last thing on Micky's mind now. 'Can you look at Buster, Dr Beth?' he asked Beth tremulously. 'His foot looks awful.'

'Oh, Micky. . .' Beth stooped over the little dog. 'You know I'm not qualified as an animal doctor. Can it wait? The new vet's due to arrive tonight.' And about time too, Beth reflected thankfully. She had her hands full with Illilawa's human population, but for months

now even such matters as the local hens' failure to lay
had been her responsibility.

'I don't think it can wait.' Micky lifted the little dog's
pad for her to see and Beth's eyes widened in horror.

The dog's pad was stripped almost to the bone. The
surrounding fur had been chewed back, making a
sickening wound. Beth dropped to her knees as the
enormity of the injury became clear to her. Gently she
ran her hands over the whimpering pup, her gaze caught
by the little dog's pain-filled eyes.

'Oh, no,' she whispered. 'Oh, my dear! What on
earth happened?'

'He got caught in one of my dad's rabbit traps,' Micky
told her, his voice filled with unshed tears. 'Buster's
been missing for nearly a week. I've walked the island
looking. Then today. . .today Fred Hastings brought
him back. He's been on his land.'

Beth frowned, her skilled fingers feeling the skeletal
body of the little dog. 'Did your Dad set traps on the
Hastings' place?'

'No.' The tears suddenly spilled over and the small
boy shoved a grubby fist across his eyes. 'Fred won't set
traps. We've got a paddock half a mile on the other side
of the Hastings' place. Buster must have dragged the
thing from there.'

'Oh, Micky. . .' Beth lifted the unprotesting dog
across to lie in her lap and stared down helplessly at the
mess of his pad. The limpness of the small body filled
her with foreboding. What on earth could she do?

Maybe the kindest thing would be to put Buster out
of his misery as quickly as she could, she thought
bleakly. Then the pup's big brown eyes looked up, the
disreputable tail gave the faintest trace of a wag and
Beth was lost.

'Micky, the new vet's due to arrive on today's flight,'

she said, and her voice wasn't quite steady. Was it cruel to raise the boy's hopes? She glanced at her watch. The plane had been due to land half an hour ago. Maybe the vet was already here. Once again she looked down at the pad. To do anything at all would require anaesthetic, and she hadn't a clue of the dosage required for such a frail animal. 'Maybe we should just settle him into my laundry, and wait,' she said helplessly. 'Has he eaten anything?'

'He had a couple of laps of water,' Micky gulped. 'He wouldn't have anything else.'

'OK. Let's not try to give him any more,' Beth told him, making her voice deliberately firm. Micky seemed close to breaking down completely. 'If the vet needs to anaesthetise him. . .'

'But will the vet really come?' Micky asked anxiously. 'Dad said he was supposed to come on last week's plane and he didn't.'

'I know.' Beth frowned. They had received a curt telegram saying Dr Ewan Thomas had been unavoidably delayed. The island had been waiting for months to find a vet after the last one left without notice. The tiny island was only just capable of supporting a veterinary practice, so Beth had no false expectations about what sort of person Ewan Thomas was likely to be. Illilawa had suffered a run of hopeless vets, and Dr Thomas was likely to be another. Still, he was qualified, so maybe he could do something for Buster that she couldn't.

She glanced at her watch again and then up to the sky. Dark storm clouds were scudding over the island. It had been a gloriously calm autumn day, but the run of fine weather was at an end. Even now the wind was rising.

'Have you seen the plane?' she asked Micky. The plane from Melbourne serviced three islands in Bass Strait and was often delayed. If these storm clouds had appeared before the plane had taken off from the neighbouring island, then it would have stayed where it was. Dr Thomas wouldn't appear until the storm was over.

'The plane went over while I was walking here,' Micky said anxiously. 'I heard it land.'

'Then Dr Thomas may be on his way here now,' Beth told the little boy. 'I'll ring Jake out at the airport.'

'I bet the vet doesn't come,' Micky whispered, his voice breaking. 'They never come, or if they do come they're useless. And the last one was so drunk my dad said he didn't know a cow's tits from its tail. If you can't fix Buster. . .'

'Hush now, Micky,' Beth told him, and she placed a hand on his heaving shoulders. 'We just have to hope that Dr Ewan Thomas is a different sort of vet.'

It seemed that Dr Thomas was at least on the island. Jake, the airport caretaker, answered Beth's phone call on the second ring. 'Yeah, he's here, Doc. If you want him you'll have to come and get him, though. I can't leave the airstrip.'

'Why not?' There was one flight a week to Illilawa. Jake usually locked the tin shed that served as the island's air terminal and drove back into town as soon as the plane left.

'This weather is why not,' Jake said morosely. 'There's a yacht overdue from the mainland and they're making an air search. Should be called off soon, 'cause this wind's getting too damned strong to stay out, but if there's search planes still in the area I gotta stay here. I'll bring Doc Thomas in later.'

'No,' Beth said slowly, looking down to where Micky was settling Buster on to a pile of old towels. 'I want him now. At least, I do if he's competent. Is he OK, Jake?'

'Dunno,' Jake said dryly. 'Seems an improvement on the last one. At least he's not drunk yet.'

Beth sighed. Her dinner looked like being a non event. 'OK, Jake,' she said wearily. 'I'll come out and get him. Just make sure he stays sober till I get there.'

Fifteen minutes later Beth pulled her car to a halt in front of the air terminal and looked around. The building seemed deserted. It was close to dark now and the wind was almost gale-force. Beth shivered in her thin cotton frock and made her way quickly to the door. The weather on the island changed so quickly it was impossible to predict, and now she was cold to the marrow. She'd left in a hurry because she was worried about Buster, but she should have taken time to grab a sweater.

Jake was sorting piles of cartons in one corner of the shed but there seemed no sign of the new vet. As Beth entered, Jake straightened and touched an imaginary cap.

'G'day, Doc,' he beamed. 'Jeepers, you're a sight for sore eyes.' His smile slipped a little. 'Your Dad'd be so proud. . .'

'He'd think I was stupid,' Beth said, and her voice was more harsh than she intended. It was only two months since her father had died and the pain of losing him was still an aching void. 'He'd tell me to go home and put a sweater on.'

'It's a rough night, all right,' Jake agreed. 'I just hope they found them beggars in the yacht. A couple and a baby. Went out from the mainland two days ago and haven't been heard of.'

Beth flinched. The seas around Illilawa were notoriously treacherous. A small yacht out in this storm would be in real trouble. 'Are they still searching?' she asked.

'They've called it off for the night now,' Jake grunted. 'I just heard. The planes can't stay up in this. Another half-hour and I'll close up. I could have saved you the trip out here.'

'I want the vet as soon as I can,' Beth explained. She looked around. 'Where is he?'

'Outside, taking a walk,' Jake said morosely. 'Real talkative, he is. Hasn't said half a dozen words since he got here.'

'Oh, Jake.' Beth dug her hands into the pockets of her loose frock and wrinkled her nose. 'Outside, in this! Is he. . . Is he normal?'

'Wouldn't be normal to take on this job,' Jake said bluntly. He smiled ruefully at Beth. 'You only came because your Dad was here. What normal person would leave a good practice on the mainland and come across to this wind-blasted place?'

'You came,' Beth retorted and the old man grinned.

'Case proved,' he smiled. 'I been told I was crazy since I was knee-high to a grasshopper.'

Beth laughed but shook her head. 'Really, Jake. Does he seem. . . Does he seem like he can at least take a bit of the load from my shoulders? I haven't a clue about veterinary medicine and I'm so sick of trying to figure out what's wrong with cows and chooks.'

'Well, as I said,' Jake said bluntly, 'he's sober at the moment. What more can you ask?'

'I'd ask for a competent vet.' Beth shook her head hopelessly. 'I'm fed up with the incompetent practitioners who think of this island as a retreat from the world. If this man turns out to be a drunk or a lunatic or a. . .'

'Or a what?'

Beth spun round in the direction of the new voice. The blast of wind around the tin walls had disguised the sound of the door opening, but the stranger's voice cut across the wind like a whiplash.

Unlike Beth, Ewan Thomas was dressed for the weather. His faded leather jacket, its collar turned up to deflect the biting wind, protected his lean, hard figure from the worst of the elements. As he stood against the door-frame, his cold eyes sardonically watching the two before him, Beth's first impression was of overwhelming bitterness. It was there in his eyes—in the way he surveyed her, as if he had seen her like before and had been unimpressed.

At close to six feet, Ewan Thomas was maybe four inches taller than Beth, and a little older. His dark, chiselled features were world weary for someone who, Beth guessed, was in his early thirties. Jet-black, wind-whipped hair added to the impression of brooding surliness, and Beth groaned inwardly. Here was a man with a chip on his shoulder. What was he escaping in coming to Illilawa?

'Or what?' the man demanded again, his eyes watchful. 'A drunk, a lunatic or what?'

'I'm sorry.' With an effort Beth summoned a smile and walked toward him. 'You must be Dr Thomas. Welcome to the island. I'm Dr Sanderson. Beth Sanderson.'

'I thought there was no other vet on the island.' Ewan Thomas' voice was as warm as a chunk of ice.

'Beth here looks after human ills,' Jake volunteered. 'She thought she'd collect you, seeing I was held up.'

'Kind of her.' Ewan's mouth twisted into a smile that didn't reach his eyes. 'Brave, too, if she thought I'd be drunk.'

'I didn't think you'd be drunk.' Beth flushed crimson. 'Of course I didn't.'

'She knew you wouldn't be,' Jake interjected helpfully. 'She told me to keep you sober till she got to you.' Jake chuckled, enjoying Beth's discomfiture. 'And I did,' he added virtuously. 'I didn't even offer the man a beer, Doc.'

Beth groaned inwardly but kept her smile fixed firmly to her face. The man before her looked familiar. Where had she seen him before? Those deep, brown eyes — the wide mouth and chiselled jaw and the harsh, sculpted cheekbones. . . Surely she had met him?

She must be mistaken. The man was looking at her as if he had never seen her before and wasn't enjoying the experience now that he had. He shrugged, as if he were no longer interested, and turned to pick up two big carry bags by the door. 'Well, if I'm not to be offered a beer, then maybe you could take me somewhere I can find one,' he said coldly. 'I'm ready if you are, Dr Sanderson.'

They didn't speak as they walked back out to the car. What a way to start a professional relationship, Beth thought ruefully as she helped Ewan Thomas store his bags in the back of her car. This was a disaster. Even if the man only lasted until the next plane trip off the island, she needed him. Buster needed him! She was going to have to find some means of communication.

'Dr Thomas, I'm really sorry if what you heard offended you,' she said softly as she gunned the motor into gear and turned the car towards home. 'Of course I wasn't expecting you to be drunk.' She cast a nervous glance across at the man's expressionless face and bit her lip. 'We've had. . . We've had a couple of disasters in our last two vets, and Jake and I were just hoping for better things. It was rude of us to talk about you.'

Ewan was silent for so long Beth thought he hadn't heard. Outside the car, the rain had started to fall in earnest and the headlights were two shimmering columns slicing through the night.

'Apology accepted,' he said at last and his voice was still expressionless. Beth frowned. What on earth was eating the man?

'We're neighbours,' she smiled, refusing to be intimidated. 'Your cottage is next to mine on the headland near the town. The island committee has prepared it for you with everything you might need.'

'But not beer in the fridge.'

'Of course there'll be beer in the fridge,' Beth snapped, her resolution to be pleasant slipping. 'I told you, Jake and I were talking of the last two vets to try out the island. We weren't talking of you.'

'But you do expect there'll be something wrong with me.'

Beth hesitated and looked sideways at his forbidding features. He was staring out into the driving rain, his face set and hard.

'There's always a reason why people come to Illilawa,' she said gently. 'I hate to say it, but often it's because they can't cope on the mainland.'

'Why are you here then? Couldn't you cope?'

The rejoinder was so harsh that Beth gasped. She bit her lip. 'I came because my father lived here,' she managed.

'So that makes you OK?'

'Oh, for heaven's sake!' Beth's patience broke. The man was a surly bore. 'Look, there may be all sorts of reasons why you're here. Maybe you're a famous painter who's looking for landscapes to paint. Or maybe you just don't like people. As long as you are prepared to do your job I don't give a damn. But you'll find life a bit easier for all of us if you're at least prepared to be civil.'

'I'm quite prepared to be civil, Dr Sanderson,' he said coldly.

'Just not friendly.'

'That's right.'

Beth nodded and concentrated on the road for a moment, chilled by his tone. Finally though her curiosity got the better of her. 'May I ask why not?'

He flashed her a look of pure annoyance and Beth winced. She wasn't used to encountering such dislike. The chill she was feeling deepened and she was left with a sense of desolation. Since her father died she had been alone on this island — as alone as seemingly this man wanted to be. The islanders held her apart — the Doc, they called her and even the island's young men seemed to treat her as a doctor and not as a rather lonely, but attractive young woman. Beth's professional friendships from her training hospital days were remembered and bitterly missed, and here was another person telling her very clearly that her friendship wasn't wanted.

Maybe he sensed — or even saw — the desolation in her eyes, because, unaccountably, his voice softened. It was a nice voice, Beth thought, rich and resonant with a trace of a Welsh lilt. 'You're right in that I came here for a reason,' he said quietly. 'I came to be by myself. I don't want people.'

'Not ever?' Beth's voice was startled.

'No.' He shook his head into the gloom.

'You sound dreadfully unhappy,' Beth said softly, and faced again into the night.

There was a long silence. She had gone too far. She'd be lucky if this man spoke to her again for the duration of his stay on the island.

'So do people make you happy, Dr Sanderson?' Ewan demanded suddenly.

'They can.' Beth thought back to her father and her eyes filled with sudden tears. 'They have.'

'But not now,' he said harshly, hearing the tears in her voice. 'And the pain's worse because you've let yourself be involved, isn't it, Dr Sanderson?'

'Maybe it was worth it,' Beth whispered, refusing to be goaded to anger. 'It's a grim life without people to love.'

They drove on in silence. The rough dirt-track was awash with the driving rain, and Beth drove with care. Her vehicle was four-wheel-drive, as were all of the island's cars, but the wheels still slid underneath them. The road followed the cliff edge on the west of the island and a fast skid could mean catastrophe.

It was hard to concentrate with Ewan Thomas sitting beside her. His physical presence was unnerving. It was as if he was staring at her, Beth thought bitterly, knowing he was doing no such thing. She felt exposed.

Why had she said so much? She had exposed herself to this man and exposing her feelings would achieve nothing. Ewan Thomas didn't want friendship. He wanted nothing but to be left alone.

Unaccountably, the sense of desolation deepened and it was all Beth could do not to weep. Then she glanced out to the black of the ocean and her desolation was forgotten. A faint orange flare splashed colour across the blackness. For a moment Beth thought she had imagined it. She took her foot off the accelerator and slowed. There was nothing there.

'What's the problem?' Ewan frowned.

'I thought I saw a flare. . .out to sea. . .'

Ewan swung around to stare into the blackness. 'There's nothing.'

Beth nodded and turned back to the steering-wheel. Then she shook her head and drew the car to a halt. It was an odd thing to imagine, and there was a yacht missing.

'I have to check,' she told the man beside her. 'I can't leave without checking.' She opened the car door and the rain slammed in against the cotton of her frock. She gasped.

'You're mad,' Ewan told her. 'There's nothing out there but miles of sea and a roaring gale.'

'If there's nothing out there then I'll get cold and wet for nothing,' Beth snapped angrily. 'But if there's a boat in trouble on the rocks down here then we're the only people who can help. I know you don't give a damn about other people, Dr Thomas, but I'm not so callous. Not yet, at any rate.'

It took Beth only seconds to get what she needed from the back of her car. Her car served as the island ambulance as well as the doctor's car, and was equipped for emergencies. There was a massive flashlight for accident work at night. Beth grasped it and staggered as she felt its weight.

'I'll carry it.' Ewan had obviously decided to humour her and was out of the car as well. He took the floodlight from her and Beth relinquished it thankfully.

'You'll get wet,' she warned him.

'Not as wet as you.' He frowned at her totally unsuitable clothing. 'Do you have a coat?'

'No. And I don't want yours,' she said quickly, as she saw what he intended. 'I'm soaked through already and the coat will just keep the water in. There's a path near here where we can get down to the beach.'

'Can't we just set the floodlight up on the cliff?'

'If there's a boat on the rocks below here, then they'll be below the line of the cliffs,' Beth said. 'To get close enough to the edge to look down is impossible, especially in this weather. The cliff edge is eroded underneath and unsafe near the edge.'

'So we have to go all the way down?'

'Yes.' Beth grabbed a couple of coils of rope and slammed the doors shut. 'Let's go.'

'Are you sure you saw a flare?' It was Ewan's turn to question Beth's sanity now and his tone told her that that was exactly what he was doing.

'No, I'm not sure,' Beth snapped. 'But I might have, and I know there's a yacht missing from the mainland. That's enough to make me check.' She started running.

CHAPTER TWO

IT TOOK ten minutes to clamber down on to the rocky stretch of shingle below the cliffs. Normally, this was a wide, sandy beach but the tide was close to full and the big sea drove the water even higher.

The floodlight was on a tripod. Seconds after they reached the beach Beth had set it up and was steadying it, focusing its strong beam out to sea. Her hands were trembling as she tried to run the light in sweeping lines across the rocks.

'Let me,' Ewan said harshly. He grasped her shoulders and moved her aside, then methodically started searching.

The driving rain made visibility almost zero, even with the big light. Beth put her hands above her eyes to keep her from being blinded by water, and strained to see along the white beam of the light. There was nothing but rocks and ocean. Nothing. The light moved slowly back and forth. For all Ewan thought this was a figment of Beth's imagination, he was taking care. He started at the left side of the bay and worked carefully, carefully across. Nothing. And then. . .

Ewan had seen it too. Before Beth could call out, the light moved back to the point it had just passed and stopped.

The yacht was wedged hard between two rocky outcrops. They must be holding her down too, because it was almost submerged. As Beth watched in horror, wave after wave broke across her, streaming water across her deck and across the rocks around the boat.

Despite the rain, Beth could make out people aboard, two figures clinging desperately to the rails on the side of the yacht. As the light from the floodlight struck them, one of the figures raised a hand in a futile gesture of appeal, and then lowered it fast to grip again as the sea washed over them.

'Dear God,' Ewan breathed and for the first time his voice had lost any trace of coldness and hostility. Like Beth, he was caught in the horror. 'What the hell. . .?'

Beth shook her head. This was grim and she knew it. Beth's father had spent his life as a lighthouse-keeper on islands as remote as Illilawa, and Beth had been brought up to the sea. She stared out at the trapped yacht, her mind racing.

'I think the boat should hold there,' she said faintly. 'The rocks that they've struck are holding her steady and the rail is out of the water in any but the worst washes. We should have time to get help.' She made to turn but Ewan grasped her shoulders and swung her around to face him.

'What are you doing?'

'I'll radio for help,' she said, pulling against his hands. 'There's a radio on the car. The boys will bring the lifeboat around from the harbour.'

'Will they be able to get in close enough to take them off?'

'They should,' Beth told him. 'There's a clear run from outside the bay and they can shoot a line over. The water on the far side of the rocks is fairly deep. I don't think. . . I don't think we can reach them from the beach.'

'OK.' Ewan's voice was clipped and decisive. 'What's the frequency of the radio?'

'It's already set,' Beth told him. 'Just pick up the handset and speak. But I'll. . .'

'I can move faster.' Ewan was already moving away. 'Where do I tell them to come?'

'Carter's Bay. South point.'

Ewan nodded through the rain and he was gone.

Beth turned back and stared out to sea. How long would the lifeboat take? It would be more than five minutes before Ewan reached the clifftop. Then there'd be ten minutes at least for the boat to be launched. Another ten minutes to bring the boat around the headland—maybe more in this weather. . . Could the people desperately clinging to the yacht hold on that long?

They would have to. Beth adjusted the floodlight again, straining to see. The figures were still there, clinging for their lives. Beth turned back to the cliff, but Ewan was already out of sight in the dark. Then, as she turned back to look at the yacht, Beth froze. What was illuminated in the strong beam of the floodlight was the stuff of nightmares.

The yacht was no longer safely wedged between granite outcrops. The rocks had released their fragile hold. As Beth watched in horror, the yacht slid silently forward, nose first into the tossing sea. Seconds later, the figures splayed forward and were lost to view.

For two long minutes Beth thought they were lost completely. She strained until her eyes hurt from looking. The boat settled forward, its bow now completely submerged, but with the rail on the stern just visible between waves. Then as Beth strained despairingly to see through the rain and the sea spray, she saw them again. Somehow the boat's occupants had managed to stay with the rail and move back to the only part of the boat now out of water. They were holding desperately to the stern rail. Beth could hardly make them out

between waves. As each wave struck they were lost to
view, as the surging rush of water washed over them.

They couldn't stay there for long. It was only a matter
of minutes before they were washed from their precari-
ous hold. Beth cast a frantic glance down at her watch
and closed her eyes in dismay. There was still half an
hour before high-tide. The waves would get bigger and
bigger until the yacht's occupants were drowned. She
looked back at the battered occupants of the yacht. It
was a miracle that they were holding on now.

Ewan would still be halfway up the cliff. Beth wondered briefly if he had seen what had happened, but
rejected it. Ewan was climbing the headland without a
torch. He wouldn't be looking out to sea — not if he was
concentrating on going as fast as he could. Beth was on
her own.

She stared down at the ropes in her hands. Could she?
She was a strong swimmer, but in this weather. . .

There was no other chance for the people on the
yacht. With a sickening jolt Beth accepted it as fact. If
she didn't do something, and do it fast, then they would
drown. Even while she was thinking, Beth was knotting
the two ropes together, giving her maximum length, and
staring round for somewhere to tie the end.

There was a huge log just above the high-water mark,
washed there in another wild storm. Beth didn't hesi-
tate. She ran, and looped the rope around its width,
scraping her hands on the rough bark as she fought to
get the rope underneath the huge trunk.

It would hold. One end of the tree was buried in the
sand and it was solidly immovable. The thought gave
Beth comfort. She hauled her sodden dress from her
body, shrugged off her shoes, looped and knotted the
rope around her waist and ran into the surf.

She had never swum in such a wild sea, and, if she'd

had time to consider, Beth would have rejected her actions as lunatic. As the first of the breakers struck her, Beth almost gave up then and there. The power of the sea was enough to knock the breath from her body. Then, in the instant before the next breaker struck, she looked forward along the line of the floodlight and saw the outline of the yacht's stern, still illuminated in the fixed floodlight. The figures were sagging against the rail and the sight gave Beth the impetus she needed to breathe deeply and dive through the next wave. She could get there. She must!

The swim seemed to take forever. The power of the water was surging against her, driving her in every direction but that which she wanted to take. As each breaker struck she dived deep to escape its wash, but the power of the water was still enough to drive her backward.

Beth had swum since she was tiny, and now everything she had ever learned in the water came back to her. All she needed was more strength. 'Please,' she was praying over and over again under her breath, and in the end she didn't know what she was praying for. 'Please let me reach the boat. Please let the occupants of the yacht still be there. Please let me take my next breath. . .'

And then the surge of water rolled her hard against solid rock. Beth choked as the unexpected movement drove her under, but as she surfaced she saw she was within ten yards of the yacht. She dived hard away from the rock and reached out towards the trapped boat. Three strokes. More. Another breath. Another, and then she had hold of a rail under the water and it was the most welcome thing she had ever felt.

Now it was just hand over hand, trying to breathe between waves, trying to work her way around the boat to the stern, where, if luck was on their side, the people she had seen from the beach would still be clinging. She felt forward again and her hand met something soft — something that moved convulsively and gripped.

It was a woman. Beth could hardly make her out in the dark and foaming surf. The woman was too exhausted to acknowledge Beth's presence by more than that clutching hand. She was near the end, dragging back against the pull of the water, but she was still clinging for dear life. And past her was a man, holding the rail with one hand and with the other clutching a sodden bundle as if his life depended on it.

'Aren't you going to pipe me aboard?' Beth yelled above the roar of the sea, but neither responded to her black humour. They knew she was there but they were both past talking. The boat beneath them shifted fractionally against the rocks, and for one sickening moment Beth thought it would slide right under. If it did before she got these people ashore then they would all drown. There was only the yacht to attach the rope to. She had no illusions as to what would happen to them all without a fixed lifeline. This rope was their only hope. Already, she was looping it through a cleat at the base of the rail. It took all her energy, having to stop three times while waves surged over her. She pulled it up, taking all the slack until it was a tight line to the beach. Let it hold, she whispered under her breath. Let it hold.

'OK,' she yelled, as she surfaced after fixing the final knot. 'You have one chance, and that's to go hand over hand along the rope to the beach. If you get there before the yacht sinks then you'll live. It's your only chance.' She was yelling in gasping phrases, between each wash of the water. 'The slower you are, the more you risk, and the person behind can't go faster than you.' Beth bit her lip. Already she had serious doubts as to whether either of the two had the strength to make it.

The two didn't move. For a moment Beth almost gave up. 'If you go back now you can save yourself,' her mind whispered insidiously and she thrust the thought aside with anger. She had to get them moving!

By now Ewan would be back on the beach. Ewan Thomas. . . The knowledge of his presence at the other end of the rope gave her a sudden, inexplicable surge of comfort. Why? She hardly knew the man and what she did know she didn't like.

She knew that he was strong. Strength exuded from the man in waves, strength of body and strength of character. If he was on the beach bullying these people to make it the last few yards through the pounding surf of the shallows. . .

He would be there. He would be there and waiting for Beth to drive herself, and these people before her. The thought was like a fist in the small of her back, shoving her forward. She put her hand on the woman's arm, pulled it forcibly from the rail and on to the rope.

'You first,' she yelled. 'Move!' She shoved the woman forward, away from the dubious security of the rail. Beth saw the woman take one agonised look back towards the man and then start moving, hand over hand towards the distant beach.

'Now you,' Beth yelled and could have screamed with frustration as she saw the man shake his head. With a supreme effort he lifted the bundle and Beth saw what he held. It was a baby.

Her mind went coldly blank for all of ten seconds. Now what? The man could hardly go hand over hand and still hold the child. Even now. . . Even now he was struggling to hold the child and still retain his grip on the rail. Instinctively, she reached forward and grasped the bundle from his arm. 'Go,' she screamed at him. 'I'll bring the baby. Go!'

He made one futile gesture of protest, but he was beyond argument. He would be lucky to make the beach at all, much less carry a child to safety. Beth swung backwards and gestured to him to pass. He went without a word.

And what now? Another wave slammed into Beth and, with only one hand to hold the rail, she was flung back against the deck. She had to do something, and do it fast.

The child was wrapped in some sort of shawl. Something soft. . . Was it still alive? Beth wondered, but, as if in answer to her thought, the tiny body stirred. From its size it must only be weeks old. What on earth were these people thinking of to expose this little one to such a risk?

There would. . .there must. . .be time for questions later. Beth put her leg around the rope she had fixed to the beach and twisted her ankle twice, looping the nylon around her leg in a biting hold, and then shoved her arm through the rail. Now she would be held, or she hoped she would, while she tied the shawl.

Somehow, and afterwards she could never figure out how she did it, Beth knotted the shawl around her neck and shoulders by each set of two corners. The baby was now encased in a cocoon hanging above her breast. Heaven knew what sort of condition the child was in, but it was the best she could do. Beth tried to make her mind think of the next step — the next course of action — as her hands once again regained the dubious safety of the rail. She could hang there until the lifeboat came, she thought desperately, and then the yacht shifted again and Beth knew she had to go.

How on earth would the baby stay alive? Beth's mind

whirled in panic and then the yacht shifted again and lurched sickeningly. There was no choice. Beth took a deep breath and moved forward, hand over hand along the rope.

If she hadn't had the baby it would have been hard enough in that driving sea, gasping and choking for breath as the sea surged around the thin nylon rope. Beth's hands were burning moments after she released the rail, but it didn't tempt her to release her grip of the cord. She had to grab tighter, dragging herself up after each movement to give the child at her breast a chance of life.

'Breathe, baby,' she whispered to herself, feeling the lead weight move slightly against her. Was it her imagination or could she feel the faint heartbeat of the infant next to her body? The thought gave her impetus to pull herself higher, ignoring the burning pain in her hands. 'Breathe, baby.' It seemed to take so long. How had she ever swum so far? The beach was a faint pinprick of light — the source of the floodlight. Beth was hauling herself along its beam, lurching to safety.

It was too far. The baby was a dragging burden around her neck. The sea washed over her again and again. It would be so easy to let go — to slip down into the sucking sea and not bother. Her hands hurt so. And her lungs. . . Her lungs were screaming their need for clear air. 'Oh, little one, I'm sorry,' Beth whispered brokenly. A breaker pounded full around her, and the surge of the last wave driving back from the beach hit her full in the face. Beth let go of the rope with one hand, swinging wildly from the other.

And then she was gripped. Somehow her wildly swinging body was steadied and her free hand was placed back on the rope.

'You can do it,' a man's voice yelled, and through her

haze of pain and exhaustion Beth recognised the faint
Welsh lilt. 'Come on, girl. Twenty yards. No more.
Move.' A strong male body came around her, pushing
her past him on the rope. 'I'm right behind you,' he
yelled. 'Move, Beth. Move!'

'I can't.' The words weren't uttered — just thought —
and they had no effect on the man behind her. He was
pushing her, his hands ensuring each of her hands found
their grip. As she gripped the rope, she was pushed
forward again, her burning hands forced to lift and
move on.

'Come on, Beth. Move. Move those hands. Once
more. Again.' Heaven knows where he was finding
breath to yell in that wild surf, but his voice was all
around her. 'Come on, Beth. You can do it.'

And then another breaker pounded her and, as she
was flung forward, her feet touched sand. The next
wave knocked her from her feet but Ewan was there to
pull her upright. He was in the shallows and it no longer
mattered about the rope, or about trying to stand. She
was in his arms and he was striding through the shallows
to set her down beyond the reach of the hungry sea.

The baby. . . Even as Beth's body met the blessed
solidity of sand she was fumbling at her neck. 'There's
a baby,' she sobbed and her words were no more than a
hacking, choking cough but Ewan understood. As she
fought to lift the cocoon he pulled her hands away,
twisting the loop of shawl up and over her head. He
knelt beside her as he pulled the wool from the tiny
body. The child was limp and lifeless in his grasp.

From somewhere close Beth heard the sound of a
woman sobbing, but she hardly took it in. She tried to
kneel up, but her knees wouldn't hold her. 'Is it. . . Is it
dead?' she managed.

'There's a pulse.' Ewan laid the child back on Beth's

breast, using her soft skin as a base to work. His fingers were swiftly searching the tiny mouth. Around them, tongues of surf were still reaching. The waves were ignored. They were in less than an inch of water and there was no time to get further up the beach.

Beth lay back, knowing she was beyond being of assistance. It was up to Ewan. . . She felt him clearing the child's airway, but hers was still so full of water she felt sick. Then Ewan lifted the child up in his two large hands. His mouth covered the tiny face and he breathed.

The roar of the sea seemed to recede as Beth stared anxiously up. Beth had been trying to breathe normally, but now her breath was held. The woman's sobs broke off as well, as if she knew that there was only the next two minutes between life and death for the little one in Ewan's hands. Ewan breathed and breathed again. The waves ran in and out, sucking the sand in channels from around Beth's body. Beth strained upwards into the dark, her heart whispering silent prayers. Please. . . Please. . .

And then there was suddenly no need for prayers. The sodden bundle in Ewan's grasp shifted slightly. Ewan's face lifted away from the child's mouth. For a long moment he stared down at the baby. Even the sea seemed to still, waiting.

A tiny feeble wail rang out into the night.

It was too much for Beth. She dragged herself to her knees and pushed her head down, but nausea washed over her. Turning aside she retched, and retched again, and then, as the worst of the sickness passed, she wept.

'It's OK, Beth.'

Ewan had left her while the sobs racked her body. Dimly she was aware of him moving between the other shadowy figures on the beach, stooping to return the child to his frantic mother. The baby's thin wail faded to silence, and then Ewan returned to lift Beth bodily higher onto the beach, away from the tongues of surf. 'It's OK,' he repeated, holding her strongly in his clasp. 'They're all safe, Beth. Thanks to you there's no tragedy.' His voice shook suddenly, and he pulled her closer as he lowered her on to the sand, trying to stop the trembling of her body with his strength.

'I. . .'

'Don't try to talk. There's no need. Even the child looks none the worse for wear, though he could do with being warmer. His parents seem to be suffering from shock and hypothermia, but they'll live.'

'I should see. . .'

'I've done all there is to be done. We wait now.'

And then there were shouts and torches and suddenly there seemed to be people everywhere. Ewan didn't move. He sat, holding Beth to him, giving curt directions and answering questions but not moving. Slowly, the worst of Beth's tremors eased. Her breathing came back to normal, and she looked around her.

The scene seemed almost normal — a group of people clustered on a stormy beach, as it seemed on the many nights Beth had spent fishing with her father. There were the man and the woman, huddled together, and several locals now with blankets and lanterns. Out to sea there were distant lights as the lifeboat rounded the headland.

'They might have been able to hold on until the lifeboat came,' Beth whispered and Ewan shook his head.

'The yacht slid right under more than five minutes ago,' he said, and Beth wondered at the gentleness in his voice. 'The rope snapped just as we came out of the shallows. If you hadn't made that crazy effort. . .' His voice broke off.

Beth stirred in his arms and reluctantly pulled away. His hold was infinitely comforting. She would stay here all night if she could, cocooned against his warmth and his strength. She couldn't. She was the only doctor on the island. Somehow she had to make her numbed body move.

Ewan released her as she struggled to rise. To her surprise he also seemed reluctant to lose the comfort of the hold. He'd had almost as much of a shock as she had, Beth told herself. What an introduction to the Isle of Illilawa! And then she realised something else. If he hadn't come. . . If Ewan hadn't moved along the rope to reach her then she would be dead. She had no illusions as to what would have happened after she released the rope.

'Thank you,' she whispered, as she pulled out of his reach. 'You saved my life.'

He shook his head, his hands still on her arms as though reluctant to relinquish the touch.

'Compared to you I did nothing,' he said roughly. 'Where the hell did you learn to swim like that? And to tie knots like that? I spent my time waiting thinking the rope would come undone from your waist any minute.'

'My father would have come back to haunt me if my knots had slipped,' Beth told him, dredging up a smile. She grimaced, recalling their earlier conversation. 'Now there's something that's been gained from a lost love.' She turned away and rose stiffly to her feet.

The cove was becoming crowded. It seemed every Illilawa local had turned out for the excitement.

'The radio call was put through to the pub to get the boys for the lifeboat,' Matt Hannah told her. Matt was a local farmer and self-appointed head of the voluntary coastguard. As Beth emerged from Ewan's hold he had come towards her, proffering blankets. Beth accepted one with gratitude, though it was already wet from the driving rain.

'We'd better get these people off the beach,' Beth said shakily. 'I don't want their hypothermia any worse.'

'We're bringing stretchers down now,' Matt told her. 'Do we take 'em to the clinic? Enid's got it open in case we need it.'

'I think you'd better.' The clinic was a small building attached to Beth's surgery which served as the island's hospital. 'The baby's going to need an X-ray to check his lungs.'

'Are you going to be able to do that?' Matt asked anxiously. He peered through the rain at Beth's white face. 'It seems to me that you've done enough for one night, Doc.'

'I can help if necessary,' Ewan told Matt, coming up behind them. 'If I can X-ray animals, I can give a baby an X-ray.'

'We guessed you'd be the new vet,' Matt said, turning to grip Ewan's hand. 'Welcome to the island. Bit of a torrid welcome, I'd say. We'll have a shindig to welcome you properly when all this fuss dies down.'

'I don't want. . .' Ewan said uncertainly.

'You don't want a welcome tonight,' Matt finished for him, beaming broadly. 'I can understand that, though a hot rum toddy mightn't go astray. What a night! And what a pair the two of you make! I dunno that I'd have been able to get that lot off the yacht, and that's the truth. Even if we'd been able to put the lifeboat behind in time, it would have been a cow of a job to get them off. Especially the babe. . .'

Beth was no longer listening. She had turned away to

where the pathetic little group sat huddled on the sand behind her. They were covered in blankets and they looked like waifs from the sea. The stretchers arrived while she watched and she crossed to where they sat.

'We'll get you off the beach now,' she said softly, kneeling before them. 'Are either of you injured in any way?'

'My hands. . .' The woman was weeping, clutching the blanket-wrapped baby to her as if it were still in danger of being dragged away. 'And my legs won't hold me. But we're alive. I can't. . . I can't believe it.'

The man reached out and clasped Beth's hand. 'Thanks to you,' he said unsteadily. 'Thanks to you.'

Beth shook her head. 'Let's get you somewhere warm and dry,' she told them. She signalled to the men with the stretchers.

'I. . . I can walk,' the man said, staggering to his feet. 'I don't need. . .'

'It's quite a climb,' Beth told him. 'And our emergency service people here need the training. They spend hours practising on life-size dummies. If you two people act as a couple of real victims — I mean patients — ' She smiled, pointedly correcting herself ' — I promise I won't let them do bandage practice on you.'

'Aw, gee, Doc,' one of the stretcher bearers said in mock exasperation. 'Can't we use just a few rolls of Elastoplast?'

'Maybe you can if he doesn't get on the stretcher willingly,' Beth grinned, and raised a general laugh. The mood on the beach was light-hearted with relief. This coastline had been the scene of so many tragedies. It was lovely to snatch a happy ending for once.

'And what about you, Doc?' the stretcher bearer asked. 'Matt told us to bring down three stretchers.'

'I don't need a stretcher.' Beth's legs were like jelly,

but she was refusing to give in to her exhaustion. 'Thank you, but no.'

'She doesn't need it.' It was Ewan's increasingly familiar soft Welsh lilt. Once again Beth felt Ewan's arms. In one sure movement he swept her up to cradle her against his broad chest. 'Let's go,' he said roughly. 'I'll carry Dr Sanderson.'

'Let me down,' Beth gasped. 'I can walk.'

'Did you mention something about Elastoplast?' Ewan said drily. 'It seems to me that it might be you who is needing it.'

The men on the beach laughed approvingly. Beth gave one futile struggle and then subsided. The feel of his arms was enough to keep the terrors of the last hour at bay. Why, she didn't know. It was enough that it did.

'Just don't drop me,' she muttered self-consciously.

For a long moment there was silence. Ewan stood looking down at her head beneath his chin, his dark eyes enigmatic in the light thrown by the scores of lanterns now on the beach.

'I won't drop you,' he said softly and strode forward towards the cliff.

CHAPTER THREE

THE next half-hour passed in a mind-numbing blur. Somehow, the occupants of the yacht were settled into the clinic. Beth dried herself off as best she could, sought for a second wind she couldn't quite find and attended to their needs. Enid, one of the clinic nurses, had reached the hospital before the patients, but she lacked confidence to do anything other than minor procedures. There was no one else to examine them.

It was the baby Beth was most worried about. The child had been unconscious when it was pulled from the water, and pulmonary oedema had to be excluded.

The child was indeed tiny. 'He's six weeks old,' the young mother whispered. Enid was helping the woman into warm clothes and bed while Beth bent over the baby. 'My husband organised to spend a couple of days at our holiday-home with a client. We planned to be there by yesterday. Only. . .'

'Only I persuaded Robyn to come out around the islands,' her husband said bitterly. He was towelling himself off, wincing at the feel of the fabric against his bruises. 'We spent longer than we should down here, and then yesterday there was no wind at all and we just sat. We've a small motor but not enough fuel to take us all the way back to the mainland. Then, when the wind finally came up it turned into a storm. We tried to run for the harbour here but. . . Well, you saw what happened.'

'Couldn't you radio for help?' Beth asked quietly. 'The alarm has been out for you since this afternoon.'

The man shook his head. 'I had trouble with the radio and took it in last week to be fixed. It wasn't ready and I wasn't prepared to wait. I. . . Maybe in retrospect it was a bit foolish.'

Just a bit, Beth silently agreed, her painful hands tenderly towelling the tiny body of her child. They had a heating pad in the cot and the heater in the clinic was turned up to full. Beth wrapped the now sleeping baby warmly and let him be. She wanted him solidly warmed before she did anything else.

'You've been very lucky,' she said quietly. She pulled the covers over the baby and walked out of the room. The X-ray would have to wait until the child's temperature was back up to normal.

Ewan was waiting, lounging in an armchair in the waiting-room. She had told him to go home. Ewan had listened politely and stayed where he was. 'When you go home, Doctor, then I'll go home,' he said politely. 'I agree you're needed, but I don't have to like it. You should be in bed.' Now he stood as she came toward him.

'I'll drive you home,' he told her.

Beth shook her head. 'My cottage is only next door,' she said wearily, 'and yours is the one just on the other side. I can't go home yet. The X-ray equipment is in the other room and the heater there is not very efficient. I don't want to unwrap the baby for the X-ray before he's completely warm. Enid can help with the X-ray. There's no need for you to stay.'

'Enid is your nursing sister?'

'Yes.'

'Then Enid can look after things for a few minutes,' Ewan said firmly. 'I'll walk you next door and you can shower and change. You're still soaked to the skin.'

'I took my wet clothes off,' Beth protested.

He raised his eyebrows. 'So I see,' he said dryly. 'You've put a very efficient white coat on. What I want to know is what you're wearing underneath. Either wet clothes or soggy knickers, Dr Sanderson.'

Beth choked on a chuckle, looked up and flushed crimson. Ewan Thomas was looking at her in a way that suggested he could see all the way through to where she definitely did have damp knickers and bra still attached.

'Well, so are. . .' Beth started defensively and then broke off. It wasn't true. Ewan was clothed in dry moleskin trousers and a warm, bulky sweater.

'I had an advantage,' he grinned. 'My clothes were in my bag in your car. While you've been ministering to your patients, I did a quick change.'

'Lucky you,' Beth said dourly, her flash of humour dissipating. Her hands were starting to throb and she was still cold to the marrow.

'So, let's go,' Ewan told her. He held open the door and the wind blasted in. 'Now.'

Beth hesitated and then nodded. If she didn't get warm soon she would collapse where she stood. The wind blasted through the door and she cringed at its feel.

'You want to be carried?' Ewan asked gently, and Beth shook her head.

'I'm fine,' she lied.

She had forgotten Micky and his little dog.

Beth's house was in darkness. Ewan carried a lantern from the clinic, and lit the way as Beth opened her back door. Micky was asleep, spreadeagled against the door to the laundry, his white face drawn and strained even in sleep.

'Micky!' Beth let out her breath in dismay. How could she have forgotten the little boy? She dropped to the floor and took the child's hands between hers. 'Micky, love. Wake up. I'm back at last. Oh, Micky. . .'

Micky stirred, his eyes opening a little and then wider, clouding with confusion. Then he remembered.

'Buster,' he whispered fearfully, and turned away.

The little dog was still alive. As Micky touched him, Buster stirred feebly and his tail moved. He was growing weaker, though. Beth's heart contracted as she turned to Ewan and briefly explained what had happened. There was no mistaking the signs that the dog was dying.

Before she had finished, Ewan had lifted the small dog and was examining the frail little body. As Beth finished speaking, he nodded.

'To think I came to this island for a quiet time,' he said drily, his dark eyes intent and his fingers gentle. 'What on earth have I let myself in for?'

'Are you. . .are you really a vet?' Micky asked tremulously.

'I really am,' Ewan assured him, his gaze coming up fractionally to meet the frightened boy's.

'And you're not drunk?'

Beth drew in her breath. Her eyes flew to Ewan's, waiting for the explosion. To her amazement, none came. Ewan's brown eyes creased into laughter.

'I'm not drunk,' he said gently. 'Though this damned island might drive me to it yet.' Then his gace dropped again to the little dog. 'Micky, Buster is very, very sick. We can't save this leg. Will you still love Buster if he has three legs?'

'Is it too bad to save?' Micky gulped.

'It's too bad,' Ewan agreed. 'Can you smell that sickly-sweet, rotten smell? That's what's called gangrene. The leg's dead. The infection from it is making Buster sick. The only chance we have of saving Buster's life is to take the leg off.'

Micky nodded again. 'My grandpa's only got one leg,' he said stoutly. 'We still think he's OK.'

'And Buster may be OK too,' Ewan told him, 'although it's too soon to make any promises. If he makes it through the operation, he'll still be able to run and hunt and keep you company. We're going to have to operate soon, though. This infection is going to get worse until we take off the leg.'

'It's OK with me, then,' Micky agreed. 'I just want him to be well.' He rubbed his eyes, suddenly looking very, very young. 'Only. . .only I don't have. . . I don't have very much money for an operation.'

Beth held her breath. Micky's parents eked out a paltry living on a subsistence farm and there'd be no money to spare for a pet dog's veterinary expenses. She couldn't say that now, though. Not in front of Micky.

'I might be able to do a deal, then,' Ewan said slowly, as though considering. 'I could trade you something for the operation. Would you consider trading every one of the traps you and your Dad use?'

Micky frowned. 'What — all of them?'

'Not one less,' Ewan told him. 'That's my charge for full veterinary care.'

'I. . . They're my dad's traps.'

'Then how about telephoning your dad and asking if he agrees? Does he know where you are?'

'I guess not,' Micky said and hung his head. 'The telephone's been ringing and someone came to the door a while ago. I reckon it was probably Dad looking for me.' He took a deep breath. 'I didn't answer 'cos I thought he'd make me go home.'

'Well, ring him now,' Ewan told him firmly. 'Get his agreement on the price of the operation and then tell him he can come and take you home. Dr Sanderson and I will take good care of Buster from now on.' Then, without raising his voice, Ewan's tone changed. 'And you, Dr Sanderson, can go and stand under a hot shower for fifteen minutes and then get yourself into warm clothes. I have need of an anaesthetist and I don't want one who's fainting from the cold. Move.'

'Yes, sir.' Beth and Micky spoke as one.

To do as she was told was bliss. Beth stood under the steaming hot water and let her mind wander. The water stung her blistered hands but the pain was nothing compared to the wonder of the hot water.

To do what she was told. . . For months — well, for years — the heavy mantle of responsibility for the island's health had been on Beth's slender shoulders. She had come to Illilawa two years before, when her father had become ill. Illilawa was to have been his last post as a lighthouse-keeper before he retired. When his cancer had been diagnosed, however, he had written to Beth and told her of his decision to stay.

'If any place can heal me, this island can,' he had written. 'And even if it can't, there's no point in me coming to the city. I've never lived in a city and I don't intend to die in one.'

Beth had agreed. Her mother had died when she was tiny and since then, until the time she went to medical school, she had lived in the country's most remote places with her father. She had been in the city since university but she hated it. She had almost been relieved that her father needed her, and she had no choice but leave the city as well.

She had grown to love Illilawa, a remote, windswept island off the south coast of Australia, but the responsibility of such a solitary practice weighed heavily on her. In her first week on the island a fisherman had died from a ruptured aneurysm. Beth had been powerless to help, and, fresh from a large teaching hospital where the man might have had a chance to be saved, she had almost left the island there and then.

'He would have died even faster if you hadn't been here, girl,' her father told her. 'Do what you can to help, but accept you have limitations.'

It was a hard lesson to learn and Beth was still learning it.

And now. . . Now it seemed as if she might have some useful professional help. A vet. . .

'I wonder if he could do an anaesthetic for me?' she said out loud, thinking of the possibilities of a competent assistant in an emergency. 'I don't mind doing his cows and dogs if he could do my appendices.'

She shook her head, giving a wry smile. She knew nothing about Ewan Thomas yet. He had seemed surly and rude. Just because the night's events had shaken him out of his surliness didn't mean he would be different tomorrow.

'But he didn't charge Micky,' she whispered, and the knowledge warmed her. There hadn't been a vet on the island in Beth's time there who wasn't intent on making the maximum amount of money in his power. And Ewan was different. . .

How different? Beth shook her head helplessly as the warm water streamed over her breasts. She was just hoping desperately that he was competent. . .

'I don't care how surly the man is,' she said defiantly to the shower-rose above her head. 'As long as he's competent. . .'

She was lying. The knowledge wafted through her tired mind like an insidious mist. She did care how surly Ewan Thomas was. That smile. . . He had smiled down at Micky and his face had transformed—from a man who wanted nobody and held himself cold and aloof, to a man whose eyes reflected kindness, care and compassion. Beth wanted to see that smile again. And suddenly—desperately—she wanted that smile to be directed at her.

'You're exhausted,' she muttered into the steaming water. 'For heaven's sake, Dr Sanderson, pull yourself together. You're reacting like a schoolgirl with a crush.'

The image of the smile stayed with her, though. It wouldn't leave. She dried herself slowly with the memory of that smile for company.

Micky had gone when Beth emerged from her shower. She pulled on jeans and a warm sweater, towelled her hair dry as best she could with her red raw hands and made her way back to the laundry. She found Ewan scrubbing down the laundry bench, surrounded by equipment he'd obviously either brought from next-door or unpacked from his bags. For a moment Beth was puzzled as to why he didn't operate in the little vet surgery at the back of his cottage and then realised that it would be cold, dank and unsterile after months of disuse. He might as well make the most of what she had here. At least it was warm.

'Micky's dad came to fetch him,' he told her, without looking up from his task.

'Did he agree to your price?'

'He didn't have much choice.' Ewan's voice was grim. 'It was either that or break his kid's heart. Or pay my fees, which I assured him would be exorbitant.'

Beth smiled and bent over the limp form of the little dog. 'I don't think you're as bad as you like to make out, Dr Thomas,' she said softly.

'I never said I didn't care for animals,' he told her roughly. Ewan finished scrubbing and turned to look down at Buster. 'Poor little devil. If I had my way traps would be made illegal.'

'Will he make it?'

Ewan shook his head. 'I don't know.' His gaze turned to rest on Beth's white face. 'I'm going to have to operate tonight, though, and I need help. Can Enid or anyone else on this island besides you do an anaesthetic?'

'No.'

'What the hell do you do in emergencies?' Ewan snapped.

'I watch people die,' Beth retorted, her voice suddenly savage. She shook her head. 'That's not. . .that's not quite true. Usually we can get help from the mainland.'

'Unless the weather's bad.'

'Yes.'

Ewan reached down suddenly, and gripped her forearm. Pulling her to stand before him, he turned her palms over. The skin of Beth's hands had blistered, burst and rubbed to raw and painful wounds. Ewan grimaced.

'Let's get a dressing on these,' he said softly.

'I don't think I can give an anaesthetic if you dress them.'

'I'll leave the fingers free.' He shook his head. 'God knows, Beth, you should be in bed. You should be over at the clinic yourself as a patient.'

'I'll go to bed when we're finished,' Beth said wearily, 'and not before.'

Ewan looked up at her pallid face and his wide mouth tightened. 'You're quite a woman, Dr Sanderson.'

Beth shook her head. 'Let's leave the woman part out of this,' she said tightly. The feel of Ewan's hands on her arm was doing strange things to her. 'For now, I'm a doctor and there's work to do. Let's get the baby's X-ray done, and then see what we can do with Buster.'

To Beth's relief the X-ray showed the baby's lungs almost clear. 'It's nothing short of a miracle,' she said softly, looking down at the film. Ewan stood beside her and nodded his agreement.

'A night of miracles,' he agreed gravely and Beth's gaze flew up to his face. Once again the cynical tone had sounded in his voice.

'You don't think so?'

He smiled then, a fleeting half-smile that was self-mocking. 'Of course I think so, Dr Sanderson,' he told her. 'I'm having trouble believing it. All we need now is to return to Buster and find him up walking.'

That would have taken more than a miracle, Beth thought sadly as they returned to their four-legged patient. It would be miracle enough if he survived the night. She looked down at the limp form and shook her head.

'Can he stand the anaesthetic?' she asked dubiously.

'I don't know,' Ewan admitted. 'But that leg's rotten and if we don't take it off the infection will kill him. I wouldn't mind guessing he'll be dead by morning without the operation, so I don't see that we have a choice.'

It was a grisly procedure — one that Beth would have done anything to avoid. She worked on the automatic pilot she and most young doctors learned during long nights in Casualty at their training hospital. When exhaustion took hold there was always some way to keep going. The only thing she had never learned to do was to make sound decisions when exhausted. When exhausted, defer to someone else's judgement, she had learned.

And here, for the first time on Illilawa, she could defer to someone else's judgement. There were no decisions here for her to make. Ewan told her exactly what to do, and Beth's automatic pilot responded appropriately.

She was aware enough to respond to what Ewan was doing though and there was a part of her singing inside. Ewan Thomas was a skilled and caring vet. His fingers moved over the little dog with meticulous care. He couldn't have given the wound more thought if he had been treating a human patient. He told Beth what he was doing as he worked, keeping her mind from dwelling on the horrors of the night and the ugliness of the dog's wound.

'I've taken it right off,' he told her. 'In a human I guess you'd try and leave a stump to fit a prosthesis, but this little mutt will manage fine on three legs.' He frowned. 'He seems to be coping. I think we can ease off the anaesthetic now. If we give him any more I think we might do more harm than good. Another three minutes and I'll have this sutured.'

Five minutes after that the thing was done. Buster had a dressing in place over the wound and a drip inserted to replace fluid and to administer intravenous antibiotic. Finally Ewan strapped the little dog's mouth.

'Because he'll wake before I will,' Ewan said, 'and what's the bet he'll try to see what I've been doing?'

'He'll be too weak for a while,' Beth protested. The mouth-strap looked grotesquely unnecessary.

'Don't you believe it,' Ewan smiled. 'He's a tough little terrier. Rid of the source of infection, he'll be up and about before your bruises from today have faded.'

'So you think he'll be OK?'

Ewan nodded. 'He's breathing strongly. If he was going to die, chances were his heart would have given out under the anaesthetic. But we made it. A hundred-per-cent success rate for tonight, Dr Sanderson.'

Beth tried to smile but didn't quite succeed. To her horror she felt tears of exhaustion slipping down her cheek. She turned away but not before Ewan had seen.

'And now, bed,' he said quietly. 'Now, Dr Sanderson!'

'I. . . Your cottage. . . I should show you where to go.'

'I'm not going anywhere tonight,' he told her. 'My patient is in your laundry and I don't want to move him, and if there are any problems at the hospital then I want to be the one who's called and not you.'

'But you're a. . .'

'A vet,' he finished for her. 'And I've been told over and over again that veterinary medicine is remarkably similar to paediatric medicine. The only one of your charges who might cause problems is the baby, and if I'm out of my depth I promise I'll wake you. The sofa here looks fine. Throw me a blanket and a pillow, Dr Sanderson and leave me to it.'

'But. . .'

'But what?' His dark eyes rested on Beth's exhausted face. 'Leave you to cope? If that phone rings tonight you won't wake and you know it. Professionally, you have no choice, Dr Sanderson.' For a moment his eyes narrowed, reflecting the cynicism that Beth had seen earlier. Much earlier. It seemed like weeks ago since she had seen that look. 'And you needn't worry about rape or pillage, Dr Sanderson. I've put all that behind me.'

Beth looked curiously up at him through exhausted eyes. 'No love, no friendship — and now not even a spot of rape or pillage. What is there left, Dr Thomas?'

'What else indeed?' he said coldly.

Beth shook her head. The sofa looked small for Ewan's large frame. The cottage only had one bedroom and Beth had used the sofa while her father was alive,

but it was small even for her. Besides. . .this man made
her feel. . .

She wasn't sure how he made her feel. She only knew
that the thought of him sleeping in the next room made
her distinctly uncomfortable, regardless of his lack of
interest in rape or pillage. 'I think it would be better if
you went home,' she said quietly.

'And I think it would be better if you stopped
arguing.' Before she knew what he was about, his hands
came out and gripped her. Once more she was swung up
against him. Cradling her like a child against his chest,
Ewan strode forward, pushing the door of her bedroom
open with his foot. He walked firmly across to the big
bed and deposited her gently on its big patchwork quilt.
'Now,' he said in a voice that brooked no opposition.
'Are you going to undress and go to bed with no further
argument, Dr Sanderson, or am I going to be forced to
do it for you?'

Beth gasped. She looked up at him and there was a
trace of laughter behind the steel-eyed determination.

'I. . . I'll undress myself, thank you,' she managed.

'Very wise,' he said, and left her to it.

Beth woke to weak winter sunlight streaming in over
her coverlet. Sunlight. . . She gasped and sat up, grab-
bing her watch from the bedside table. Ten p.m., it told
her uselessly. Its immersion in salt-water the night
before had done it no good at all. She glanced out of the
window. It must be much later than the time she usually
rose. There was her clinic. . .

She pushed back her covers and rose to her feet, only
to fall back as the events of the night before made their
effects known. Every muscle screamed a protest.

She had to get up. There would be patients at her
regular morning clinic, and the family in her little

hospital might need her. Beth took a deep breath, told herself she was imagining the worst of her muscle pain and rose to sitting. As she did, there was a firm knock on the bedroom door and Ewan Thomas walked into the room.

He was carrying breakfast. The smell hit Beth before she saw it — the fragrant smell of brewed coffee and another smell she hadn't known since childhood. Porridge? All of a sudden Beth's aches and pains receded as her stomach stirred appreciatively. When was the last time she'd eaten? Too long ago, her stomach told her. Her eyes flew to the tray Ewan was carrying and then higher to where his cool brown eyes were surveying her with a hint of humour.

'I didn't miss my guess, then?' he smiled. 'Your ordeal hasn't damped your appetite.'

Beth smiled shyly up at him, her empty stomach giving a strange lurch as she registered the humour in his eyes. He looked more enigmatic than ever this morning, rugged up for the wind in a thick polo neck sweater and cord trousers, his tanned face dark against the light wool of his sweater. His eyes rested on her appreciatively and Beth made a sudden grab for her bedclothes, dragging them up to cover the scantiness of the nightgown covering her breasts.

'I am hungry,' she admitted softly, flushing a becoming shade of pink. She looked uselessly at her watch. 'I . . . I shouldn't stop, though. I'll have patients waiting.'

'No patients.' Ewan placed the tray down on her bedside table and perched himself on the foot of her bed. It was a peculiarly domestic gesture, proclaiming an intimacy about them that didn't — shouldn't — exist. Beth gave herself a mental shake. Where was the surliness she remembered from the night before? 'Your clinic has been cancelled,' Ewan continued. 'The whole island is agog at Dr Sanderson's exploits of last night. Enid's put a note on the clinic door saying anyone with urgent problems can contact her in the first instance and me in an emergency. If they can prove they won't live till lunchtime without your intervention then I'll allow them to disturb you.'

'But. . .'

'No buts.' Ewan smiled again, his wide mouth twisting wryly. 'For today you're a heroine, Dr Sanderson. Lie back and enjoy it.'

Beth tried to smile up at him, and then turned her attention to her tray. It was a defensive gesture. She couldn't keep looking at those eyes. 'Did you. . .did you cook this?' She looked down at the plate. 'Or did Sandra. . .?'

His grin deepened. 'Sandra being the lady who does the hospital breakfasts and who's currently over at my cottage pursing her lips at my unmade bed,' he smiled. 'No, Dr Sanderson. I made the porridge. Sandra is shocked to the marrow. I hate to say it, Dr Sanderson, but your reputation is in tatters.'

Beth gave a rueful smile. 'It doesn't matter,' she said slowly. 'My reputation has been a trifle too squeaky clean of late.'

'The local farmers below your touch?' Ewan said drily and Beth flushed. There was no mistaking the insulting cynicism in his tone.

'That was mean,' she whispered. 'What have I done to you to deserve that?'

Ewan stared down to where Beth's fingers toyed with a slice of toast. There was a long, awkward silence. Apologise, Beth was silently demanding, but no apology was forthcoming.

'Our patients are doing fine,' Ewan told her finally, his eyes resting on Beth's bent head. 'Even Buster. . .'

'He'll make it?' Beth kept her eyes on the plate. She was finding it difficult to concentrate on the food.

'Even Buster.'

Ewan rose, his eyes still and watchful, giving away nothing of what he was feeling. He stood looking down while Beth attempted to eat. The silence stretched on and on. Beth concentrated on eating the porridge without spilling it and tried desperately to think of something to say. The lovely creamy porridge slid down effortlessly.

'I thought you were Welsh,' she managed. 'Your accent. . .'

'I am Welsh.' He smiled again and his eyes lit. 'Why?'

'Porridge?'

'My mother was pure Scots. I was born and raised in Wales, though, and came out when I was seventeen.'

'Why?'

'My parents were following a dream,' he said briefly. 'Australia. Land of endless sun and golden opportunities. Only dreams have a habit of turning to nightmares.'

'Is that what happened to you?'

Ewan didn't answer. He stood, looking down, the laughter completely gone from his eyes. 'I'll leave you, then,' he said finally, roughly. 'Go back to sleep.'

Beth forced herself to meet his eyes. 'Thank you for my porridge,' she said quietly. 'Is. . .does your cottage have everything it needs?'

'Everything,' he told her. 'Including enough food for an army. The island committee obviously thinks I need more feeding than you think you do. Your refrigerator, on inspection, held bread, cheese, a limp lettuce and half a litre of milk. Hardly soul food, Dr Sanderson.'

'I meant to shop yesterday,' Beth said defensively.
'I. . . I was too busy.'

'Rescuing shipwrecked mariners and sewing up dogs.'
Ewan nodded. 'The committee president came around
an hour ago to see if there was anything I needed. I told
him I wanted two casseroles in your refrigerator by
tonight, plus provisions to match mine.'

'There was no need to do that,' Beth protested. She
shook her head. 'I can look after myself.'

'You don't seem to be doing a very good job of it.'
Ewan walked to the door and stood looking back down
at her.

Beth looked down to where the traces of her lovely
porridge lay in her bowl. 'Well, thank you for doing it
for me,' she said softly. 'For this morning. . .for this
morning, I do appreciate it.'

'For this morning, I don't mind doing it,' Ewan
told her. He walked out, and the door closed heavily
behind him.

CHAPTER FOUR

THE remainder of the day passed in a hazy blur of sleep. Rather to her surprise, Beth did sleep again. Her sleep was fitful, interspersed with memories of the night before, but the horrors were supplanted by another more powerful image. Whenever the horrors became too much for her, in her dreams there were strong arms reaching out to grasp and hold, and carry her to safety. To carry her to warmth and security and. . .

And what else she didn't know. Beth only knew that those arms were enough to hold the nightmares at bay.

When Beth finally stirred, she felt as if she'd been on holiday. To sleep the whole day away. . . She rose and stood under the shower, washing her soft brown curls and letting the hot water soothe away the aches from the night before. She dressed in jeans and warm sweater. It was five-thirty in the afternoon and the storm outside didn't sound as if it intended abating for the next twenty-four hours. Beth saw little point in dressing up to go over to the clinic. Skirts and clinical white coats had no place on Illilawa in weather such as this.

She made herself a cup of coffee, noting that Ewan had cleaned up scrupulously in the kitchen. There was no sign of him or his three-legged little patient. He must have taken Buster across to his cottage, Beth decided, and was aware of a sharp stab of disappointment.

What were you hoping? she asked herself crossly. That Ewan Thomas be seated in my easy chair reading the island's weekly newspapers?

Yes, she admitted to herself truthfully. Yes. . .

It didn't make any sense to be feeling this way, she chided herself, drinking the remains of her coffee too fast. Ewan Thomas had been kind this morning and there was an end to it. He was a loner—she'd be a fool if she couldn't see that. He wanted no friendship from her, and she could want nothing from him. 'Nothing,' she told herself crossly, and wondered why her voice sounded suddenly forlorn.

Enid came out to meet Beth as she entered the foyer of the small clinic.

'We didn't want to see you today, Doctor,' the middle-aged nurse said severely, her kindly eyes taking in Beth's face. 'Eh, Beth, you still look like you could use another day's sleep.'

'I'm fine,' Beth said firmly. 'But what about you? You haven't been here all day?'

'Of course not,' Enid reassured her. 'Coral came over and relieved me this morning and I've only just come back.' She grinned. 'I had to fight for the privilege, too. Coral reckoned she was staying on until she managed to get a look at the great Dr Thomas!'

'The great Dr Thomas?' Beth said blankly.

Enid stared. 'Surely you know who he is,' she said flatly. 'I'll admit when I heard Dr Ewan Thomas was coming to the island I didn't connect him with the TV programme, but once I saw him. . . You must have seen him, Beth. He's on the telly every second night compèring that vet show—*Two by Two*. . .'

'*Two by Two*. . .' Beth thought back to the last time she had watched television—an age ago, she thought, in the time before she had come to the island. Illilawa boasted one television for the entire island operating via a satellite link and set up in the local pub. As the pub was a place Beth hardly visited, she didn't see television. She had watched it while she lived in the city, though — in the long night-duties when there was little else going on in dim wards. And yes, she had seen the programme — a gentle, humour-filled hour of pet care and general animal talk. How to choose your pup. How to care for your canary's impacted toenails. The merits of various breeds of cat. It was a fun, light-hearted show which every age group seemed to enjoy and suddenly Beth had a clear mental picture of the laughing, gentle compère of the show. It was Ewan. That was where she had seen him before. The gentleness had gone from his eyes now, though, and the laughter.

'What on earth is he doing here?' she gasped, and Enid beamed.

'I can tell you that too,' she said roundly. 'It was in my favourite magazine a month or so back. Dr Thomas was married to a woman who worked on the show with him — an investigative journalist. Gorgeous, she was. Every time I saw the show I commented on it. I thought they were a lovely couple — just made for each other. Then, about a year ago or maybe a bit more, she took off with the show's producer. There was a heck of a fuss and the show nearly folded. It didn't, though. Dr Thomas kept it going and it got better and better. Then about a month ago he suddenly announced he was quitting. The magazine said he was going to write a book. . .'

'Write a book. . .' Beth shook her head slowly. 'I guess he's come to the right place, then.' She was silent for a minute. Was this, then, the reason Ewan Thomas looked so darned cynical?

It was none of her business if it was. Beth gave herself a mental shake, cross with herself for indulging in what seemed dangerously near gossip. All it needed was for

Ewan to walk in behind them and catch her at it again. He had caught her talking about him before. . .'How are my patients?' she asked abruptly.

'They're fine,' Enid said proudly. She smiled. 'I rang Joe down at the general store and he opened up and drove over with some formula for the babe during the night. Master Samuel woke hungry, would you believe, and his mum was sleeping like the dead. He had two big formula feeds and another two from his mum this morning. He's tough, that one.'

'It's just as well.'

Enid nodded. 'Just as well for him that you are too,' she said, her voice softening. 'Eh, Beth, you took a fearful risk.'

Beth shrugged. There seemed little point in dwelling on the events of the night before.

She checked swiftly on the little family, reassured by what she saw. The young mother seemed the worst of the three of them, her bruised face wan and exhausted against the pillows.

'I gather there's a guest-house on the island,' the father said hesitantly as Beth completed her examination. 'If it's OK with you, Doctor, we can move there until we arrange for a flight back to the mainland.'

Beth shook her head. 'You may, if you like, Mr Bource,' she said firmly. 'But I want your wife in here for another twenty-four hours at least. She had a Caesarian birth six weeks ago and her body isn't fully recovered from that. She needs bed-rest and lots of it.'

'She can sleep at the guest-house,' the man said belligerently.

'And who's going to feed the baby in the middle of the night?' Beth asked. She looked down at the man's face, assessing him for what he was. 'Will you get up, change the baby and bring him to your wife in bed?'

'I. . . I don't usually wake. . .'

'No,' Beth said grimly. 'I don't suppose you do. Unless you want your wife with complications then she stays where she is. But, of course, you're free to leave. If you'd like to go with Enid she'll show you where our telephone is. If you ring Mrs Ellen from the guest house she'll come and collect you.'

The man looked across at his wife and gave a shame-faced grin. 'Do you mind, Robyn? I just. . .'

'I know,' his wife said wearily. 'You'll be much more comfortable in the guest-house and you can start organising salvage of the boat without worrying about us.'

His face cleared. 'I can,' he agreed.

Two minutes later Beth was alone with the white-faced woman. From the sound of the voices outside the door, Mr Bource was organising more than just his accommodation from the telephone in the foyer. Beth looked down at the woman on the bed.

'I think you might be able to sleep better now,' she said gently. 'And that's what you need.'

'I. . . Yes,' Robyn Bource whispered. 'He. . . He can't keep still. He always has to be doing something. Even the week I came home with Sam. . .'

'So this exhaustion isn't just from last night's ordeal?'

'I've been tired since Sam was born,' the woman told Beth. 'Tired to death. But John. . . John just never stops.'

'Well, he's stopped now,' Beth smiled. 'He may not like what he's about to find out. The weekly plane touched down at the island yesterday and there's not another flight for a week. With this weather there's no way a charter firm will collect you. I hate to say it, but your chances of salvaging the boat are zero. There's nothing for you to do for the next six days, Mrs Bource, but sleep. Your husband can visit you and go fishing.'

'I shouldn't say it,' Robyn Bource smiled weakly, 'but it sounds like bliss. Won't. . .won't we be an awful bother if we stay here though?'

Enid re-entered the room as the young woman spoke. She looked down into the crib where the baby lay fast asleep and beamed. 'Bother!' she snorted. 'We haven't had a newborn babe on the island for two years. This little one doesn't know how many cuddles he's in for.'

Beth left them and walked slowly back to her cottage, her face down to avoid the bitter wind from the sea. The cottage seemed lonely and deserted, although it was no more lonely than it had been at any time since her father died. She lit the fire in the kitchen stove, eager for the comfort of its warmth, and then checked her refrigerator. She smiled when she saw its contents. It held two casseroles plus a week's provisions. Someone had come in while she slept and carried out Dr Thomas's orders.

It seemed strange not to be busy. She felt lazy and ill at ease, facing what she spent her working life trying to avoid. That without her work on this island she was bereft. She was needed as a doctor but as nothing else.

She had to do something or she was going to burst into tears. Beth shook herself crossly. It wasn't like her to be lachrymose, and the feeling wasn't one she intended to encourage. A good stiff walk was what she needed — to walk the stiffness out of her joints from yesterday's battering and the loneliness in her heart from. . .

From her father's death, she told herself soundly. It wasn't anything else. She was just missing her father.

Why wasn't it the image of her father's face rising before her now, then? Why was it the image of cool brown eyes with a smile lurking just behind — a smile that was held back and bestowed only reluctantly, but was there nevertheless.

'Damn Ewan Thomas!' Beth stood and grabbed her anorak. She was going down to the beach to let the wind blow these stupid thoughts from her mind.

Below Beth's cottage was a flat shelf of shingle dropping gently to a wide stretch of rock-strewn sand. There was nothing between this beach and the Antarctic and the breakers roared in ceaselessly. It was unsafe for swimming even on the calmest day in summer, but today the gale whipped the sea up to a frenzy.

Beth loved it. She always had. Others on the island bemoaned the constant bad weather but this was how Beth wanted it. Standing before the might of the sea, she felt insignificant and small, as if her mistakes were of no moment in a greater scheme of things. The feeling was one of comfort and of peace.

Beth made her way along the rain-soaked sand, pushing into the wind. The salt spray almost blinded her. Finally she reached the point where the beach curved away to the west. Out to sea, a natural breakwater of rocks broke the rhythm of the surging water, and Beth stared in disbelief. There was a man seated on an outer rock. Ewan. . .

For a moment she thought he must be in trouble and started forward, but then stopped short. The figure was motionless, seated on the wave-swept rock. The spray was lashing his figure and it seemed as if he didn't notice.

Even though Beth couldn't see clearly through the driving spray, it had to be Ewan. There was no one on this island who'd be this crazy — to sit as if he didn't care about the dangers of the sea, to sit as if he was totally unaware of the elements. His dark, brooding figure seemed almost to weld with the rock on which he sat and Beth knew suddenly that there was no danger. The sea wouldn't shift Ewan Thomas. Two opposing forces, each implacable and each relentless in their isolation. . .

What had happened to this man to make him so alone? Beth stood staring out to sea, pondering the story Enid had told her. Was this man really running from a broken marriage — shunning the world because of one fickle woman? Had he thrown away his career because of that?

It didn't make sense. Beth shook her head and turned away, leaving Ewan to his solitude. He wanted to be alone and Beth's need for company was not strong enough to break into that solitude. She made her way further around the beach, forcing her feet forward along the wet sand, trying to drive away the crazy feelings she was experiencing with sheer physical effort.

Half an hour later Beth telephoned her neighbouring cottage. She was safely ensconced back in her now warm kitchen. Darkness had fallen outside and she saw the light come on next door, signalling Ewan's return. Beth had just taken her casserole from the oven and, on impulse, dialled Ewan's number. He answered on the second ring.

'Yes?' The tone was curt and business-like.

'I. . .' Beth flushed, feeling like a schoolgirl who was acting like a fool. 'I've just made dinner. Would you like to join me?' There was no smoke coming from the next-door chimney. Ewan's cottage would be cold and comfortless after his bleak walk.

'Thank you, no.'

Beth grimaced. She should have known. Why on earth had she bothered to ring?

'I'm sorry to annoy you, then,' she said, and her voice matched Ewan's for coldness. 'I was just trying to be friendly.'

There was no response and Beth felt her colour mounting further. Despite this morning's overture this man was an arrogant boor. Conceited, too! Where were the rudiments of good manners?

'You might at least tell me how Buster is,' she said coldly. 'I have a professional interest.'

'I told you this morning that Buster's fine.'

'He's over at your cottage?'

'Yes.' There was a momentary hesitation and Beth heard a loud banging through the receiver. 'And if I'm not mistaken this will be Micky here for visiting hours.'

'Well, what a shame,' Beth said drily.

'I beg your pardon?'

'That will be a precious few minutes where you can't savour your own company,' she retorted, and slammed the telephone back on its cradle.

Beth didn't see Ewan Thomas again for three days. Their cottages were a stone's throw from each other but their paths didn't cross, and by the end of the third day she was beginning to wonder whether it was by accident or design.

Certainly everyone else on the island seemed to have met the new vet, and wherever she went Beth heard about him. To have a new vet on the island was news in itself but to have a television celebrity was almost too much. After three days Beth was heartily sick of the discussion seemingly raised by every one of her patients.

'Oh, we are lucky, Dr Sanderson,' Beth was told by her twentieth patient for the day. 'To have someone as good as Dr Thomas. . .'

'We don't know if he's good,' Beth said waspishly. 'We only know he's good on television. . .'

He was darned good sewing up Buster, was the general consensus, as well as hauling Beth from the water when she needed it. The islanders decided that they had a hero on their hands—a famous hero—and they were relishing the idea.

'He's better-looking than on the telly,' old Mrs Cameron confided to Beth as Beth dressed the abscess on her leg. 'Don't you think so, dear?' The old lady looked down at Beth, her eyes twinkling.

'He looks like a man with a chip on his shoulder to me,' Beth confessed. 'Mrs Cameron, have you been resting this leg? I want it kept up.'

'You told me that last week,' the old lady agreed.

'I know I told you, but have you done it?'

'Well, I do take a wee nap after lunch. . .'

'Well, the wee nap is to stretch to an hour after breakfast, an hour and a half after lunch and straight to bed after dinner. Otherwise, into the clinic with you. . .'

'Says who?' Mrs Cameron smiled saucily. 'Beth, dear. . .'

'Don't "Beth, dear" me,' Beth said firmly. 'Just because I'm small and female you reckon you can ignore my orders. Don't forget that it's the island co-op that's paying both my and Dr Thomas's wages. He's therefore required to co-operate if he's needed, so if I find you not following orders I'll send our Dr Thomas around to forcibly bring you in to hospital.'

Mrs Cameron grinned. 'You know, I might just enjoy that,' she confessed.

'Don't try me,' warned Beth. 'Because I mean what I say.' She placed the last bandage in place and glanced at her watch. She had one last patient to see and then she'd promised to make a house call to the other side of the island.

The house call was to Lorna Mackervaney. Lorna Mackervaney was a lady in her late sixties. Beth visited her as often as she could, and each time she visited she worried more and more about Lorna and her gentle husband, Fergus.

Lorna and Fergus ran a small herd of dairy cattle on the coast, south of Illilawa's settlement. Fergus had inherited the farm from his father who had it from his father before him. Lorna was originally the daughter from the farm next door, and neither of them could bear the thought of shifting from the land.

Fergus, though, was the last of the Mackervaneys. With no children, and with Lorna ill, there was now no one to help with the farm. The Mackervaneys were faced with the choice of continuing to operate the farm or selling. Either choice seemed impossible.

Beth frowned as she pulled up outside the run down little farmhouse. Fergus Mackervaney was expecting her and usually he came out of the house to open the yard gate and greet her. This time, though, Beth was forced to open the gate herself and let herself through. The dogs were not there to greet her either, so the elderly farmer must be occupied somewhere else on the farm. Then, as Beth drew her car to a halt, she saw Ewan Thomas's Land Rover parked beside the dairy.

So, Ewan was here. . . Beth took a deep breath, chiding herself for her stab of inexplicable panic. So what? She wouldn't see him. She could be in to see Lorna and gone again before Ewan and Fergus returned to the house.

Lorna was in the single bed which Fergus had moved into the farm kitchen for her. She was unable to rise for long, but had fought against bed-rest until Fergus had set the day bed up for her. Here she lay and bossed her meek little husband and superintended the girl who came in to help. The bossiness had faded, though, on Beth's last few visits, and Beth was becoming increasingly concerned.

'You already have a visitor?' she smiled, noting the greyness of Lorna's face. The fingers lying flaccid on the bedcovers were white and bloodless.

'Yes.' Lorna managed a smile. Her voice was weak and breathless. 'Such a nice young man. He's herd-testing with Fergus. The co-op wants every herd done. Fergus is a bit worried about it.'

'Fergus is a darned good farmer,' Beth said roundly. 'He shouldn't have any problems.'

'It's just. . . He's so taken up with me now,' Lorna said sadly. 'I think sometimes. . . I think if I just died then he wouldn't have to worry.'

Beth sat herself down on a chair beside the bed and took Lorna's hand in hers. 'Do you really believe that?' she said gently.

'I. . . I don't know.'

'Well, I know,' Beth told her. She smiled. 'You and Fergus are one of the closest married couples I've ever seen. Not even a couple, I'd say. You're one person. Even though you're unwell and can't do the things you've done in the past, Fergus doesn't need you any less. You're his wife, Lorna, and without you he'd be lost.'

'I. . . I wish I could believe that.'

'You have to,' Beth said firmly. 'Because it's true. Lorna, if you were well and Fergus were ill — if you had to do his work for him and care for him, and your precious housework suffered because of it, then would you rather Fergus died?'

'Of course. . .of course not.'

'There you are, then.' Beth gave a decisive nod and smiled down at Lorna. 'Keep telling yourself that in the middle of the night when the world seems bleakest. Because it's true, Lorna, and in your heart you know it's true. Fergus loves you and there's an end to it. Now, let's have a listen to your chest.'

What she heard wasn't reassuring. The four-hourly salbutamol was no longer sufficient, and Beth knew it. Lorna's lung capacity was decreasing to the point where she was receiving insufficient oxygen and her body was beginning to react to the stress it was under.

Lorna had to have an oxygen concentrator. Beth mechanically completed her examination, her mind mulling over possibilities. How on earth could she get one? She had one in the clinic but it couldn't come out here to be permanently on loan. It wouldn't be a short-term loan either, Beth knew. With an oxygen concentrator Lorna's quality of life would improve and her outlook could be long-term.

Could they afford to buy one? Oxygen concentrators retailed at over four thousand dollars and a glance around the shabby kitchen told Beth that such money was just not available. If she told Fergus his wife needed the concentrator then he'd sell his soul to buy it for her, Beth knew, but besides his herd and his farm there was little else for him to sell.

You're a doctor, Beth told herself harshly. Not a social worker. Your job is to lay the options before the Mackervaneys and leave it to them to sort it out.

It'd be wrong to hand this over to a social worker and walk away, even if there was a social worker on the island, she responded to herself. I'm the island's doctor and I'm all they have.

She packed her bag, still mulling over the problem, when the sound of dogs barking frantically close to the house signalled the arrival of Fergus.

He came into the kitchen, a stooped, wiry little man, weathered to leather-brown by constant exposure to the elements. He crossed swiftly to give his wife a hug, then straightened to greet Beth. As he did, Ewan Thomas walked in behind him.

'How are you, Doctor?' Fergus said heavily to Beth, and then turned to Ewan. 'I'm sorry I came in before you, lad. I've been. . .' He turned back to Beth, his eyes pleading. 'I've been that worried about Lorna.'

Ewan's cool eyes surveyed the scene. They crossed from Beth to the woman on the bed, and back to Beth again.

Beth tried to ignore him. She really needed to speak to both Fergus and Lorna, and the last thing she wanted was Ewan Thomas as an audience, but it seemed she had little choice. 'I'd like a cup of tea, Fergus,' she said gently. 'Can I make us one?'

'I'll make it,' Fergus said brusquely. 'If you just give me a minute to wash up. . .'

'So excuse yourself, Ewan Thomas,' Beth said under her breath. 'Take yourself off.'

Ewan Thomas did no such thing. 'I need to talk to Fergus about his herd,' he agreed. 'And a cup of tea would be good. If I may?'

'Of course you may,' Lorna managed from her pillows. 'It's a long time since we had two visitors at once. Fergus, there's seed-cake in the cupboard. Mary left it this morning.'

'I'll fetch it,' Beth smiled, inwardly shrugging at Ewan's unwanted presence. 'The men can go and rid themselves of their disgusting smell.'

'It's easy to see you weren't brought up on a dairy farm,' the old man grinned. 'Nectar of the gods, that smell is, girl.'

'I think I'd prefer to stick to Chanel or Dior for my smells,' Beth grinned back. 'Or even rotten seaweed. Go and get rid of it while I make tea.'

* * *

Once again, Beth was too close to Ewan for comfort. Seated in the overwarm kitchen, a pot of tea and seed-cake before them and the sick woman on the bed behind them, the overwhelming sensation of intimacy came back to Beth. It was as if she had known Ewan for much, much longer than three days. It was almost as if he was part of her. . .

'Fergus, I'm really worried about Lorna,' Beth said gently to the elderly farmer, pushing aside the unwelcome sensations Ewan's presence was creating. 'I think you are too, and so, I think is Lorna herself.' She turned back to the bed. 'You're not as well now as you were last week, are you, Lorna?'

'No, I'm not,' Lorna sighed. 'And that's the truth of it. Maybe. . .' She swallowed. 'Maybe there's not all that long to go, Beth, lass.'

Beth shook her head, wishing desperately that Ewan weren't there. She felt so self-conscious, and surely the Mackervaneys felt it.

'I don't think you're close to death, Lorna,' she told her. 'But I do think you need more help than you're getting now.' She hesitated. 'Lorna, I'd like you to come into the clinic for a few days.'

Lorna's face set. 'No,' she whispered. 'I'll not leave here.'

'Lorna, it's for a few days only,' Beth promised. She lifted Lorna's fingers. 'Look. Your fingers are becoming cyanosed. That's because you're not getting enough oxygen. Unless we correct that, you're going to get complications that we might not be able to handle. You need to be using an oxygen concentrator.'

'An oxygen concentrator. . .'

'It's a machine which is fairly simple to use. Once your lungs are receiving sufficient oxygen you'll be much better.'

'If this machine is simple to use, can't we bring it out here?' Fergus asked.

'I only have one machine,' Beth told him. 'And I'm sorry, Fergus, but I can't leave it out here. If I need it for someone else you're too far away.'

'Well, how much does one of these machines cost?'

'About four thousand dollars.'

'Four. . .' Fergus fell silent, staring at the dregs of his cup of tea.

'If I come into hospital, when can I come home?' Lorna whispered. 'If I use this machine for a few days, will I be better?'

'I think so.'

'But then, when I come off it. . .'

'Then you may deteriorate again. But let's cross that bridge when we come to it.' Beth took a deep breath. 'I'll try and persuade the hospital committee to buy me another machine. There are other patients who could use it.'

'They'll never do it,' Fergus said dourly. 'The hospital fund's broke and you know it, girl. If the island wasn't dependent on dairying and fishing—two industries which are both in deep recession—then you might have more hope.'

'Fergus, you never know until we ask.' Beth stood up. 'But Lorna has to come in. She knows it and so do you.' She looked down at the ill woman. 'Tonight, Lorna,' she said gently. 'I told you that Fergus needs you, and he needs you alive. Isn't that right, Fergus?'

'You're not giving us much choice, girl,' Fergus said roughly.

Beth shook her head. 'I'm sorry, Fergus. There really isn't any choice to give you.'

There was a long silence. It was Ewan who broke it. He stood, lifting his cup across to the sink. 'Thank you for the tea,' he said softly, the Welsh lilt in his voice at its most pronounced. 'You need to talk to Dr Beth and I'm in the way. I'll talk to you about your herd improvements another time.' He held up a restraining hand as Fergus rose. 'I'll see myself out. And at least you've no worries about your herd, Fergus. They're as fine a lot of friesans as I've seen. I'm sure the results of the testings will come back just as you wish.'

Fergus nodded, his face set and grim and Beth knew he wasn't thinking of his herd. 'Thanks, young fella.'

Ewan nodded, cast a quick glance across at Beth, smiled fleetingly at Lorna and left. It was as much as Beth could do not to run after him. A child would have escaped this torrid situation, she thought, and run to comfort.

Why on earth was she equating Ewan Thomas with comfort? She took a mental grip on herself and rose as well. 'Now, Lorna,' she said, and her voice held a hint of a tremor. 'What do you need for a stay in hospital?'

Lorna looked up at Beth's face and her kindly eyes crinkled into a smile. 'Why, Dr Beth,' she said softly. 'You're blushing.' She grinned, distracted from her medical problems by her young doctor's obvious discomfort. 'Our new Dr Thomas is good-looking, isn't he, dear?'

'I wouldn't know,' Beth snapped. 'I haven't noticed.'

'Well, well.' Lorna's smile deepened. She shook her head. 'You know, something tells me, Dr Sanderson, that you're not being honest.'

'Lorna. . .'

'I don't say you're telling me lies,' Lorna said sagely. 'But I don't think you're telling the truth to yourself!'

CHAPTER FIVE

IT WAS late before Beth finished at the clinic that night. Lorna needed more reassurance than actual medical treatment. Once on the oxygen, Lorna's breathing eased, but her anxiety for Fergus made her restless and inclined to be feverish. When Beth finally saw her fall into an exhausted sleep she had to stop and talk with the young mother in the clinic's other bed, and her own bed was starting to seem very desirable. She walked out of the clinic door and found Ewan Thomas waiting on the low stone fence overlooking the beach.

'I thought you'd decided to stay there the night,' he said grimly and Beth flushed.

'I had to see Lorna settled,' she told him. 'Now, if you don't mind, I have my dinner to prepare and my bed to find.'

'I've made dinner for you.'

Beth's eyes flew up to meet his. 'Why?' she asked bluntly before she could stop herself.

'I want to talk to you.'

'You can talk to me now.'

He shook his head. 'I saw your car come back an hour after mine and you've been in the clinic ever since. Therefore, it stands to reason you can't have eaten and I've a casserole in the oven—courtesy of the island committee.'

Beth smiled up at him, amused by the grim 'let's get this over with' tone in his voice. 'You sound as if you're doing your Christian duty,' she said gently. 'You really don't have to.'

He shrugged and started walking. After a moment's hesitation Beth did likewise. The temptation to ignore him was there but Ewan Thomas was not a man to ignore. If he wanted to eat dinner with her. . . Well, it was one less lonely meal she would have to prepare.

Lorna's accusation came fleetingly into her head. 'I don't think you're telling the truth to yourself.' She shoved it away in anger, cross with herself for admitting there might be a grain of reason in what her patient had said.

Ewan's cottage was identical to Beth's, but as she walked in the back door she stopped in dismay. She had forgotten how bleak the little cottages really were. Ewan's cottage might have identical construction to hers but there the resemblance ended. It was bleak and spartanly furnished. The island committee had furnished it as they thought fit but they had certainly not decorated it. Ewan had added nothing.

Nothing. . . Beth looked around, searching for some sign of Ewan's personality imposing itself on the stove-warmed little kitchen, but there was none.

'Are your belongings coming by sea?' she asked. Ewan was placing plates on the bare wooden table, and lifting the casserole from the oven.

'I brought all I needed with me,' he said brusquely.

'You're not. . .you're not planning to stay for very long, then?'

'Why do you say that?' The man seemed hostile again. He placed the casserole on the table with uncalled for force and Beth jumped.

'I guess. . .well, it's not very homey, is it?' Beth thought of her own kitchen, cluttered with the belongings of her own and her father's life. Sometimes she thought she had too many possessions but when she came to throw any out she was stopped by the myriad memories associated with every piece.

'It's as homey as I want it to be.' Ewan gestured to the casserole. 'How much do you want?'

'Heaps,' Beth smiled. 'I'm starving.'

'Your permanent state,' he said grimly. 'Aren't you receiving casseroles too?'

Beth grinned. 'I am,' she told him. 'Thanks to you. I've had a casserole a day since you arrived, and I can't keep up. It's just a matter of finding time to eat them.'

'Is your medical practice too much for one person?'

Beth shook her head. 'It's not,' she admitted. 'More than one doctor on the island would be too many. I do have busy times, though, and this seems to be one of them.'

'The patients in the clinic are keeping you busy?'

Beth frowned, sinking down at the table as Ewan gestured toward the piled plate of steaming hotpot. 'Yes, they are,' she admitted. 'Mrs Bource is taking longer than I thought to recover.' She frowned. 'It's as if she doesn't want to. . .'

'Maybe she doesn't,' Ewan said, starting on his heaped plate. 'We should have salad with this.' He smiled and Beth's heart did a lilting jump at the way his face changed. 'I'll give you an apple at the end.'

'That's all I need.' Beth ate another mouthful of casserole, thinking back to the tired mother in her clinic. 'I think you might be right.'

'With a husband like that I wouldn't get better,' Ewan said drily. 'He's driving the islanders mad in his quest to salvage his boat. He can't seem to get it into his head that the thing's impossible. I'd imagine that a small obstacle to his enjoyment such as the needs of a baby would easily be ignored.'

Beth nodded gratefully. She wondered whether Ewan

Thomas knew how blissful it was to be able to talk about her patients. Ewan might be a vet but as far as Beth was concerned he was a professional colleague and she could discuss her worries with a colleague. She didn't have to be told that he would respect professional confidentiality.

She ate her casserole thoughtfully, her mind on the man before her. He was still silent and grim. Life was a hard business for Ewan Thomas, it seemed. There was little place for humour.

'You wanted to talk to me,' she said softly as she completed her meal.

'Yes.' Still nothing was forthcoming. Ewan stood and started making coffee.

'Well?' Beth's fingers curled into her palms with impatience.

'I wanted to talk to you about Mrs Mackervaney.'

'Oh.'

'She'll be OK?'

Beth hesitated. 'No,' she said at last. 'I don't think so. Not unless we can get an oxygen concentrator for her at home. She won't stay in the clinic and I can't make her. With her oxygen intake I think we'll soon be looking at complications at home.'

'Fergus is thinking of selling the farm.'

Beth's eyes flew up to Ewan's. 'How do you know that?'

'He told me.'

Beth shook her head. 'Fergus Mackervaney is a very private person,' she said at last. 'I've tried to talk to him. He shuts up like a clam.'

Ewan shrugged. 'Well, he talked to me and he's certainly considering it.'

'It won't work,' Beth said bluntly.

'Why not?'

'Because the farm won't sell.' Beth rose. 'Don't make coffee for me, Dr Thomas. I. . . I need to go.'

'It won't sell because the farm's too small?' Ewan ignored Beth's last statement and poured hot water into two mugs.

'Yes.'

'It'd solve his problems, though, wouldn't it? They could move into a smaller house and have money to spare for the concentrator.'

'I don't think Fergus would cope without his beloved farm.'

'No.' Ewan stared thoughtfully at the steaming coffee in his mug. 'No, I can see that. And he's a few years left of being physically capable of managing the place.'

'Look, this is a fruitless discussion,' Beth told him. 'Even if they find a buyer they won't find one fast enough to do any good. Lorna needs an oxygen concentrator now — not three months down the line. I'll try to get the hospital committee to purchase one for her.'

'Will you succeed?'

Beth shook her head. 'I doubt it,' she admitted. 'But it's all I can do.'

'The least you can do,' Ewan said softly. 'And Dr Beth Sanderson always does the least she can do.'

Beth flushed an angry shade of crimson. She shoved the cup back from the table. 'Thank you for the meal,' she said savagely. 'I have no idea why you brought me here, but if that's your opinion of me, then you won't see me again. Goodnight, Dr Thomas.'

He stared at her for a long moment. 'Drink your coffee, Dr Sanderson.'

Beth walked to the door. 'Thank you, but I don't want to,' she said coldly and walked out into the night.

Ewan caught her before she reached the stone fence

bordering what passed for the front-garden. He caught her arm and swung her around to face him.

'Let me go,' Beth said icily, pulling away from him.

'Beth, I'm sorry.'

She swung to glare at him. 'And so you should be,' she snapped. 'I've done nothing to hurt you, Dr Thomas, but you act as if I'm something less than human. Or is that the way you treat everyone?'

'No. I. . .'

'So, I'm singularly favoured for your rudeness and your insults. I'm honoured, I'm sure. Now let me go.' Beth wrenched backwards and stumbled. The low stone of the fence caught her legs and she sat abruptly. Ewan moved forward, his dark figure looming over her in the dim light.

'Are you all right, girl?'

'Yes.' Beth forced herself to stand, intensely aware of his body before her. 'Though you'd probably be delighted if I broke a leg!'

Ewan didn't move. He stood silent, blocking her escape.

'Beth. . .'

'Let me go. . .' Beth's voice faltered. She looked up but he was too close. The roughness of his sweater was against her. His arms came out to steady her, but they did more than steady. They held her rock-solid and then brought her hard against him. In one swift movement his head bent and his lips caught hers.

Beth hardly knew how it happened. One moment she was standing, still and confused, and the next she was being ruthlessly, demandingly kissed.

The sensation was such as she had never known. His strength was so much greater than hers that her involuntary recoil was futile. His hands held her in a grip of iron, and her lips were caught and held.

Amazement swept over her—amazement and fury that he should dare to touch her. She pulled back, but the hard, demanding mouth held her still, demanding a response, and all of a sudden the response was there. She laced her hands against the rough wool covering his chest in a futile attempt to push him away, but the scent of him caught her—the feel of the coarse wool—the blatant masculine strength. . .

Her lips quivered under his as her body warmed to his touch. Ewan felt the betraying quiver. His hold tightened and the kiss deepened, deepened until Beth thought she was drowning.

She had never felt like this. What on earth was happening to her? Her whole body was trembling to his touch and the cold of the bleak island night had dissipated into a fierce, all-consuming warmth. It was as if a fire had been kindled deep inside her body, lighting places that had never been lit—warming places that she hadn't known had been cold.

She was crazy. With a ragged gasp of disbelief she caught at the remains of her common sense and shoved as hard as she could. To her mind's relief but her body's dismay, Ewan finally responded. His hands fell from her sides and she was released.

Beth fell back, her hands rising in a defensive gesture as if to ward him off, but Ewan didn't follow. He stood staring down at her in the dim light, his face showing nothing of his emotions.

'Y. . .you're mad,' Beth whispered. 'You don't even like me.'

Ewan said nothing. His hand lifted fractionally, as if he were trying to reach her, and then fell back to his side.

'Thank you. . .thank you for dinner,' Beth managed. 'Was that a demand for payment?'

'Beth, I. . .'

He didn't continue. They stood, looking at each other in the dark. It was as if there was some invisible thread holding them fast together. Turn and leave, Beth told herself harshly, but Ewan was looking at her and she could no sooner break that look than she could fly.

It was Buster who broke the moment — Buster — Ewan's tiny patient. . . The little dog's small, warm body bumped into Beth's leg and involuntarily she looked down. What she saw there made her almost forget Ewan Thomas. Almost. . .

'Buster,' she said unsteadily and knelt down. The small dog put his tongue against the palm of her hand. He licked and licked, and Beth felt an almost overwhelming desire to weep.

Ewan had left the back door open when he had followed her. The little dog had obviously woken and followed their voices. He was struggling on three legs but he gamely kept on, his hind legs pushing themselves up in a vain attempt to jump and greet Beth.

'Oh, Buster,' Beth whispered, kneeling on the wet path. 'Oh, look at you. You're better.'

'Not better enough to be out in the cold,' Ewan said grimly. Buster's interruption seemed to have brought him to his senses — reminded him of the aloof, cold stranger he was supposed to be. He stooped and scooped the pup up from Beth's grasp as she rose unsteadily to her feet.

'He looks. . .he looks great.'

What had just passed between Ewan and Beth was too raw to even be acknowledged. Somehow, Beth had to ignore it. She shook her head as if trying to pass from some crazy dream, placed a hand briefly on the little dog's head and turned to go.

'Beth. . .'

She didn't turn back. 'Goodnight, Dr Thomas,' she managed.

Beth slept fitfully and woke before dawn. Although she was still weary, sleep would no longer come. She lay in her bed and thought over and over of the events of the night, trying to make some sense of them.

Why on earth had he kissed her? He hadn't seemed like a man wanting a light dalliance. Well, he wasn't, Beth thought grimly. Idle dalliance and Ewan Thomas were contradictions in terms.

Why couldn't he just be a friend? she asked herself, acknowledging her need for friendship.

Her body answered her. 'Ewan Thomas could never be a friend,' she whispered to herself. 'Because that's not the way I see him. Ewan Thomas is a man to my woman. My body wants Ewan Thomas.'

The thought jolted her into an even greater wakefulness. 'Damn you, Beth Sanderson,' she swore at herself. 'What on earth are you doing to yourself? This man is a loner. He's here for a short while to escape problems on the mainland. As soon as he comes to terms with the loss of his wife, he'll be off — back to the glitz of his city life.'

She was almost willing the dawn to come. Beth's bed was no longer comfortable. She tossed and turned, her body aching strangely, and finally she flung off her covers and dressed. If she was going to be wide awake she might as well accept the inevitable and do some good. A brisk walk on the beach would set her up for the day. Her body was still stiff and sore from the exertions of three days ago and a walk would loosen stiff muscles.

Beth checked the clinic briefly before leaving. Coral was on duty. She acknowledged Beth with a silent wave, gesturing to her three sleeping patients with satisfaction. Lorna's breathing was deep and steady. On the other side of the room young Mrs Bource slept a dreamless sleep, as did her son lying in the crib beside her. Despite the ordeal of the shipwreck, Robyn Bource would leave hospital at the end of the week better than she had been at the birth, Beth thought in satisfaction, reminding herself to give a lecture to Robyn's thoughtless husband before she released the woman and child to his care.

She wasn't needed at the clinic and it was four hours before morning surgery. 'You should still be in bed, Doctor,' Coral whispered to her. 'Have you had a call-out?'

'No.' Beth shrugged. 'I couldn't sleep. I'm going for a walk. I'm wearing my receiver if you want me.'

The middle-aged nurse stared. 'Going for a walk at this hour? You've rocks in your head.'

Ewan Thomas, more like, Beth acknowledged bitterly as she pulled her big anorak back on and left Coral to her patients. She had Ewan Thomas going around and around in her head and she couldn't rid herself of him.

The beach was icy, blasted by the south wind driving up straight from the Antarctic. The cold was just what Beth needed. Her body still felt as if it were on fire. She blushed over and over at the thought of her involuntary reaction to Ewan Thomas's touch the night before. Pulling her anorak closer around her, Beth set her face into the driving wind and walked.

The sand was strewn with massive piles of bull kelp, torn from the sea bed in the storm. It smelt good, clean like the sea. Later in the morning the kelp farmers would be down here with tractors, heaving the kelp on to trailers for drying and processing. Beth pushed a wide ribbon of it aside, pleased with the idea that such a massive natural resource could be utilised. Many of the medicines she prescribed had this seemingly useless weed as their base.

She walked for almost an hour before turning. The radio receiver remained silent in her pocket and Beth wasn't concerned at going so far. A track lay around the headland so if she was needed urgently someone could drive around to collect her.

Still, she couldn't keep walking indefinitely. Whatever it was that she was trying to drive from her system wasn't being driven. Beth's normally sunny nature had taken a downturn. For some stupid reason the arrival of Ewan Thomas to her sheltered little island had made her depressed and miserable.

'And it shouldn't,' she said savagely into the wind. 'He's a crazy, mixed-up male who doesn't know what he wants out of life. He's got nothing to do with me.

'So cheer up,' she told herself firmly. 'Take a hold on yourself.

'I could have if he hadn't kissed me,' she muttered. 'If he hadn't kissed me. . .

'He did kiss you. And it meant nothing. Nothing,' she reiterated. 'For heaven's sake, the man is a bitter, woman-hating recluse. He kissed you because. . .'

Because! The word went through and through Beth's head, driving away the hard physical exertion of walking against the wind on the wet sand. It drove away everything. . .

Not quite everything. Something stirred in her consciousness. Something different. . . From the corner of her vision around her all-enveloping anorak hood Beth saw a slight movement. Was she imagining it or had something stirred in the pile of bull kelp closest to the waves?

Had a seal come ashore to escape the worst of the

weather? Beth gingerly stepped over the slippery pile of kelp, bound to investigate. The need to do something other than think of Ewan Thomas was almost welcome. Water was rushing through the kelp to foam over her feet but she ignored it. Her feet were soaked to the socks anyway. A bit of wading wouldn't make them any wetter.

Something had moved. Something black and sodden and limp. . .

It was a tiny fairy penguin, struggling to find its feet on the slippery weed. The waves were battering it against the soft kelp. It washed in and out with the water and, by the look of it, was close to death.

Beth stooped to look closer. She placed a hand down to touch and the tiny beak jabbed forward. Beth withdrew her hand, smiling a little as she did it. If the penguin could still defend itself then it wasn't as close to death as she thought.

But what was wrong with it? Old or ill birds were often washed up on this shore, and Beth knew that nature had to take its course. As the daughter of a lighthouse-keeper she had stopped being sentimental about the death of wild creatures long ago.

This bird looked young, though, and plump, not the usual condition of a dying bird, and although Beth wasn't sentimental, neither was she uncaring. If she could just get a close look. . . A larger wave caught the bird and threw it forward, splashing the legs of Beth's jeans in the process. For an instant the bird rolled in the dull morning light and Beth saw clearly what the matter was.

The bird was coated with an oil-slick. Its normally water-repellent feathers were slicked down with a mat of slimy oil. Without its insulating feathers, the bird would be sodden and freezing to death.

An oil-slick. . . Beth's lips tightened with anger and her green eyes flashed. With normal diseases Beth might be tempted to let nature take its course, or even help nature on a little if nature seemed cruel, but not with this. This young, healthy bird was dying because of the crass negligence of some stupid human.

Oil. . . Beth stared down at the bird, her mind thinking of the possibilities, and suddenly she knew what had happened. The yacht. . . They had a motor on board, with a full fuel tank. This fuel would now be a slick spreading over these waters. The rough sea would have broken the slick up, but this bird must have come into contact with it while it was still a thick mat of destruction.

She should put it out of its misery now. Beth stared down at the miserable little creature at her feet and felt tears pricking behind her eyes. The fairy penguins were her favourite of all the birds. They nested in a rookery to the south of the island and Beth often made her way there at dusk to see the fat little adults waddling importantly back to their young with their day's catch. The birds delighted her. One of the last excursions she had made with her father had been to watch the penguins coming ashore. . .

So, she wasn't going to watch this little one die. If human carelessness had caused the problem then human intervention could fix it. Beth took a deep breath, pulled her anorak from around her shoulders and stooped to cover the bird with the thick waterproof material. The bird's beak could not jab through the thickness of the coat. Beth wrapped it securely, one hand finding the beak and holding it, and the other securing the webbed feet. With her wrapped parcel tucked under her arm she turned to make her way back along the beach.

It would be faster to walk along the road. Without her anorak Beth was freezing. Swiftly, she made her way up the sand, stumbling a little as the beach rose in sandy clefts to the firmer ground beyond.

It was still very early. Beth glanced down at her watch, forgetting for the moment that the thing was sitting waterlogged and useless on her bedside table. It was light, but only just. Six o'clock, she guessed. It would take her an hour's walk to get back to her cottage. The bird in her clasp gave frequent indignant struggles. Clearly he was unappreciative of Beth's offer of assistance and was upset by the indignity of his mode of transport. Beth took a firmer grasp, turned her head towards home and started walking.

She was in luck. Five minutes later a truck came lumbering up behind her with Matt Hannah at the wheel. The farmer pulled to a halt and gazed at Beth in stupefaction.

'What in blazes. . .' He stared at her open-mouthed. 'You in trouble, Doc?'

'I've just been for a walk,' Beth smiled at him. 'I wouldn't mind a ride now, though.'

'I dare say you wouldn't.' The farmer shook his head, clearly deciding she was unhinged. 'I thought *I* was up at the crack of dawn!'

Beth climbed up into the cab, blissfully conscious of the wind being blocked by the cab's solid structure. As she settled herself on to the seat the bundle in her arms gave a violent wriggle. Matt stared down, fascinated, and it was all Beth could do to suppress a chuckle. 'I've been collecting a patient,' she said cheerfully.

'Yeah?'

The chuckle broke out regardless, and Beth lifted a flap of coat to reveal some sodden, oil-stained tail feathers. 'A fairy penguin,' she said softly, her smile fading. 'And he's pretty crook.'

The farmer looked from Beth down to the bird in her arms. Visibly he took a deep breath. 'Well,' he said on a long note of enjoyment. He would relish telling this story in Illilawa's pub that evening. 'A medical emergency,' he grinned. 'I'll put my foot down. Pity I haven't a radio or we could demand a police escort.'

Matt dropped Beth outside Ewan's cottage five minutes later with enough noise to wake the dead. Rising nobly to his calling as ambulance driver, the farmer put his hand on the horn as he neared the cottage and left it there.

'Hush,' Beth told him, half laughing and half exasperated. 'You'll wake the patients in my clinic.'

'Patients in hospital will have been awake hours ago,' Matt said darkly. 'I know. You put me in there last year when I broke my leg. Sister Pike insists on patients being bathed and brushed and lying in straight lines before she'll think of breakfast. And you want this young vet in a hurry, now don't you?'

Beth shook her head, unable to argue further. As the truck drew to a halt the farmer leapt down and helpd her out of the cab as a bemused Ewan Thomas opened his back door to investigate the noise.

'Got you a patient, Doc,' the farmer told Ewan cheerfully. 'Your medical opposition's been going round the beach collecting 'em for you. She must think we're not giving you enough to do. Don't forget, you're supposed to be testing my herd this afternoon.'

Ewan had clearly just woken, pulled on his trousers and come to the door. He stood, bare-chested, his eyes creased against the biting wind as he looked across in stunned silence.

'Thank you for the lift,' Beth told Matt swiftly. She

took a deep breath and walked forward to where Ewan stood. She would rather not see this man again, and now. . . Now she needed him.

'I've a penguin,' she said slowly.

'You're soaking.'

Beth nodded. 'Only my jeans and my feet,' she said ruefully. Behind her, she was aware that the farmer hadn't moved. He was taking in every last detail of what was going on. 'Can we. . .can we go inside? You must be cold, too.' Ewan's bare chest was making Beth's voice sound odd. She was sure it was that. Damn the man for being so. . .well, so male!

Ewan nodded. He looked over Beth's shoulder to the farmer and a trace of humour lit his eyes. 'Which one's the patient?' he queried.

Matt grinned. 'Look after 'em both,' he advised.

Ewan did just that. 'Get over to your place and find some dry clothes,' he ordered Beth roughly. 'Then come back. I'll need some help here.' So once again, Beth stood under hot water at Ewan Thomas' command, warmed herself thoroughly and then made her way back over to his cottage. It was still very early. There were a couple of hours before patients would be arriving for morning surgery.

Ewan had clearly been waiting for her. He was working in the small surgery behind his cottage, and as Beth walked in she was conscious of the warmth of the place. Ewan had grabbed three electric heaters — obviously every heater the cottage possessed — and turned them on to full. Beth had donned a big sweater. She pulled it off two feet inside the door.

Ewan himself was now wearing a shirt, covered by a large waterproof apron. He was holding the little penguin expertly as he wiped oil from its feathers. He looked up briefly as Beth entered. 'Good,' he said. 'I need a vet nurse but you're going to have to do again.'

'Gee, thanks,' Beth said wryly.

'There's CDA up on the shelf over there,' Ewan told her, ignoring her comment. 'It's the powder, third from the left. Grab a box from under the cupboard and put about half the contents of the CDA in. Then, as I lower our friend in I want you to gently press handfuls of the powder on the oiled surfaces.'

Beth nodded, moving swiftly to comply.

They worked silently, each intent on their task. Ewan held the bird immobile, carefully manoeuvring it so that the worst of the oiled surfaces were exposed. The areas under the wings were the worst affected.

'She's been preening,' Ewan said grimly. 'There'll be oil in her gut. You can tell that by her condition. I took her temperature before you arrived. It's down to thirty-seven. If you hadn't found her she'd have died this morning.' He glanced up at Beth briefly. 'The oil destroys the waterproofing and insulating properties of the feathers, causing hypothermia. With oil on her feathers she'll get as cold as you would swimming in this freezing water.'

'I knew I walked for a reason,' Beth whispered, intent on her task.

'I think that's the worst of it,' Ewan told her finally. 'I can't see any more. We'll give her another going over in a few hours but if we handle her much longer we'll cause too much stress.'

'So we leave her be?'

'Not until we get some fluids into her. I want as much of that oil flushed through her system as I can. Left inside it can cause ulceration and bleeding, kidney damage and pneumonia. It'll cause dehydration in itself so we have to rehydrate.'

'I'd set up an intravenous line, given a human,' Beth said doubtfully. 'How do we do this?'

Ewan frowned down at the bird in his grasp, obviously deep in thought. 'I don't want to anaesthetise,' he said slowly.

'How. . .'

'I'd anaesthetise with isofluorane and oxygen if I had to.' He hesitated. 'It's a punt, wondering how much stress a bird can handle. Anaesthetic reduces mental stress for the bird but it stresses the body in other ways.' He shook his head. 'I think we'll take a punt and go for the oral route. Can you hold her?'

Beth nodded, shifting so that she could be handed the bird. The little penguin took the change of handler well, her small bright eyes looking up in silent wonder.

'It's almost as if she knows we're helping her,' Beth said softly.

Ewan shook his head. 'She's given up struggling. I'd be happier if she was fighting. People tend to pat sick birds to comfort them and as they quieten down they think they've succeeded. What they don't realise is that a passive wild bird is a bird very close to death. Human comfort is just additional stress for a wild creature.'

Beth nodded, watching Ewan prepare the fluid. 'What are you using?'

'Lectrade. It'll help restore a few nutrients as well.'

Skilfully, Ewan worked. His fingers slowly inserted the crop needle over the back of the bird's tongue. The little bird's eyes widened with alarm. It gave one final writhe of dismay and then lay passive as the tube passed into the oesophagus and the crop beyond. Ewan's spare hand straightened the bird's neck and the fluid ran in. He didn't stop until the fluid welled up in the back of the bird's throat and then the crop needle was swiftly withdrawn. The bird gagged and shook its head feebly, ridding itself of the excess fluid, and the thing was done.

'And now,' Ewan said, taking the bird from Beth's grasp, 'now we've done all we can do. We place her in a quiet, dark place, keep her warm and hope.'

'That's all we can do?'

'That's all we can do,' Ewan said grimly.

'Do you. . .would you like me to come over at lunch time to help you feed her again?'

'I'll contact you if I need you but I just need someone to hold her. You've a full morning's surgery?'

'Yes.' Beth stood, aware of a weird feeling of unreality. 'You. . .you'll be busy too?'

'I was supposed to be herd-testing,' Ewan said grimly. 'But not now.'

'Not. . .'

'No.' Ewan sighed. 'I'm about to gather as many able-bodied people as I can and scour the beaches. That oil-slick was thick and foul and I'd be crazy to think there'll be only the one bird affected. This one's been lucky, Dr Sanderson. I'll see if a few more can't be helped.'

Beth nodded. 'You don't. . .you don't think I was stupid trying to help?' She took a deep breath. 'I thought maybe. . .maybe I should have just put it out of its misery.'

Ewan shook his head, the harsh look fading from his eyes. 'I can't see our Dr Beth Sanderson making such a decision,' he mocked gently. He placed a finger against her cheek and Beth's face burned. 'Care and compassion a speciality,' he mocked.

Beth flushed. 'I didn't see you refuse to treat it,' she managed. 'And a penguin's no paying customer, Dr Thomas. Why are you going back out to the beach if you think I'm so stupid?'

'I didn't say you were stupid,' Ewan said softly. 'The

people who were stupid. . .' He shrugged and looked
down at the oil-stained rags on the bench. 'I'll keep
these,' he said. 'If we can salvage enough of the yacht to
prove that's where the oil came from, then John Bource
can pay for the penguin's treatment. He's more money
than sense as far as I can tell, and it's time he faced up to
the consequences of his crazy actions.'

Beth nodded. It was time for her to go. She looked up
at Ewan and then away, her colour still high. There was
a current of tension running between them that she
could almost touch. 'I'll. . . I'll see you soon,' she
managed.

CHAPTER SIX

THERE were no more live penguins to be found. Beth walked over to Ewan's cottage at lunchtime to find he had been back to feed his patient and had gone again. His surgery was unlocked, so Beth walked in and peeped into the storeroom where the little bird was recuperating. It was huddled in the corner of the room on rubber matting, looking absolutely miserable. Beth closed the door, resisting the pointless and probably harmful impulse to try and comfort the penguin, and as she did she heard the back door open. She looked around to see Matt Hannah in the back door. In his hands the farmer held the limp forms of four dead penguins.

'G'day, Doc,' he said grimly, laying the birds on the bench. Beth looked down. All four little forms were coated in foul-smelling oil.

'Oh, no,' Beth said sadly.

'And that's not the end of it,' the farmer told her. 'We've been searching all morning. The oil must have been washed in a sheet around the headland where I picked you up this morning. Doc Thomas says it must have happened the night of the wreck or just after, because we're too late to help these little fellas.'

Beth nodded, fingering the still forms. 'Why have you brought these back here?' she asked.

'Doc wants to do a post-mortem,' Matt told her. 'Wants to see just what damage the oil's done to their innards. He reckons it might help him treat the live one he's got back there.' He shrugged. 'Also, he wants to show that clown who beached the boat just what sort of damage he's done.'

Beth nodded. 'Is Ewan. . . Dr Thomas. . .still on the beach?'

'He's still looking.' Matt looked down at the limp forms on the table. 'I'm a farmer, Doc, with a farmer's attitude to animals, but when Doc Thomas told me how long these little fellas would have taken to die well. . . well, he's supposed to be herd-testing for me this afternoon but we decided to spend the day searching instead. We've found more'n fifteen — including a couple still alive but so crook Doc had to put 'em out of their misery.'

Beth smiled sadly up at Matt's weathered face. 'You're not as tough as you look, Matt.'

'Yeah, well, there's a few of us not so tough,' the farmer agreed. 'He's not alone on the beach.'

Beth went back to work with a heavy heart. The penguins of Illilawa were a delight, not only to Beth but to all the islanders. It seemed such a wicked waste.

'It makes you worry,' one of Beth's patients told her. Mrs Grey was the wife of a local fisherman, in to have a papilloma on her foot pared and treated with formalin paste. 'If the petrol from that little boat can do so much damage. . .'

'I wouldn't have believed it could do so much,' Beth agreed. She brought her thoughts forcibly back from the penguins to Mrs Grey's proffered foot. Her mind was wandering all too often these days. 'Now, Mrs Grey, let's give this papilloma what it deserves.'

Beth finished work just after dusk. The lights were on in Ewan's cottage and there were a couple of trucks pulled up out the front so Beth assumed that Ewan had all the help he needed. It was hard to resist the temptation to go and see what was happening to the little penguin she had found.

'He's still alive,' Micky Edgar told her an hour later. He dropped in on Beth just as she finished dinner, Buster firmly cradled in his arms. 'Doc Thomas phoned and told me to pick Buster up tonight. I guess he's out on a call now though 'cos there's no one there but I'll take Buster anyway.'

'I don't think Buster and a fairy penguin are very companionable room mates.' Beth smiled. 'He looks great, Micky.'

'Yeah, well, I just came over to say thanks,' Micky said shyly. ''Cos Doc Thomas said you helped operate and. . .and. . .' He looked up, took a deep breath and then buried his face in the little dog's fur. 'I dunno what I'd have done if he'd died and. . . Well, thanks,' he finished lamely.

Beth ruffled the small boy's hair and smiled. 'That's OK, Micky. I guess we were just lucky Dr Thomas arrived when he did.'

'That's what everyone's saying,' Micky told her, recovering as he backed away. 'I think. . . I think Doc Thomas is great. I think I might even be a vet.' He turned and fled into the night.

Beth stood for a moment watching Micky's small figure disappearing into the darkness. 'I think Doc Thomas is great. . .' Micky's words lingered in her mind. Involuntarily her fingers rose to touch her lips, and the remembrance of the roughness of his embrace came flooding back. Why had he kissed her? 'I think Doc Thomas is great. . .'

Micky was at the gate when something occurred to her. 'Micky!'

The small boy stopped and looked back. 'Yeah?'

'How are you getting home?' There was no car waiting and Ewan's cottage was in darkness.

'I'm walking,' he said stolidly. 'Dad's taken the truck to the cliff paddock—he's got a cow calving—so Mum said if I wanted Buster tonight I'd have to walk.'

Beth nodded. She grabbed her coat and car keys. Micky could well walk the two miles home, she knew, but it was a miserable night. 'Come on, then, Micky,' she said. 'I'll take you home.'

They passed Ewan on the coast road. His Land Rover was parked beside the beach where Beth had found the penguin, and in the clouded moonlight they could see his figure walking slowly along the beach.

'He'll never find any more live penguins after this time,' Micky said, horrified. 'What's he doing, Dr Beth?'

'I guess he's just enjoying his own company,' Beth said slowly. 'Anyway, Micky, let's not disturb him.'

Beth slowed as she neared the top paddock of the Edgars' property. Graeme Edgar's truck was a hundred yards from the road, its lights illuminating his work. Micky's father was stooped over a prostrate cow, and the cow was obviously in trouble.

'She's been having the calf all day,' Micky told her. 'Dad's really upset 'cos she's a beaut little heifer and he thinks he'll lose her.'

'Why doesn't he call Dr Thomas?' Beth frowned.

''Cos we can't afford it,' Micky said simply.

Beth nodded. She drove Micky up to the house, bade him goodbye and then drove back to the paddock. Nothing had changed. Graeme was still stooped over the cow. He looked up and watched as Beth pulled to a halt and left the car. Beth walked from the fence over to the cow, wincing at the bitter wind. She winced again as she saw what was happening. The little heifer was lying

on her side on the sodden, sandy ground, her huge
brown eyes rolling in agony. The calf was breech, its
back legs protruding from the cow's narrow pelvis.

'Oh, Graeme,' she said softly. 'How long's she been
like this?'

'A couple of hours,' he said wearily. 'I can't shift it.
Did you bring Mick home?'

'Yes.'

'Thanks, Doc.' He looked down at the calf. 'Do you
reckon. . . Do you reckon if I hook the back legs to the
truck and pull. . . I know I'll kill the calf but if I get it
out, the cow might live.'

Beth shook her head. 'No,' she said firmly. 'I know
enough about human birth to know you'll kill the cow.
She'd never stand the trauma.'

He nodded and stood. Wearily he walked over to the
truck and when he returned he was carrying a gun.
'That's it, then,' he said bleakly. 'I'll not let her suffer
any more.'

Beth put her hand on the gun in a gesture of denial.
'Graeme, Dr Thomas is just down the road. Why don't
you get help?'

'I've no money,' the farmer said heavily. 'God knows,
I want to but we've had a rotten season. . .'

Beth knelt, and her fingers moved over the hind
quarters of the half-born calf. She frowned. 'Graeme,
it's still alive,' she said.

'Yeah. Well, it won't be for long.'

'But it's a heifer. Born alive it'd be worth more than
Ewan would ever charge.'

'Yeah,' Graeme said again. 'As a grown cow, maybe.
But there's a solid chance he won't save it, and besides,
he won't send a bill for the future profits in a cow.'

'No.' Beth sat back and looked up at him. 'But what
if. . .what if I buy a part of your calf? What if you agree

to pay me Ewan's bill out of milk profits once she starts milking?'

'You're mad.' He stared down at her. 'I'm not taking charity. . .'

'OK, pay me back double Ewan's bill,' Beth smiled. 'I'm taking a gamble, but I reckon it's a fair investment.'

'You'd do that?'

'I'll double my money if she lives.' Beth smiled at the weary, dirt-stained farmer. 'Such is my faith in Dr Thomas. What I want you to do is get into the truck and find him. He's on the beach about half a mile back. Then go up to the house and bring back as much hot, soapy water as you can carry. Really soapy. And towels.'

The farmer stared down at her. 'You'd really do this, girl?'

'Get moving,' she told him, turning her attention to the cow.

Ewan's Land Rover arrived five minutes later, following Graeme's ancient truck. He pulled to a halt behind Beth's car and strode swiftly across the paddock while Graeme returned to the house for the hot water.

'Still acting as island vet?' he asked curtly and Beth flushed.

'I made Graeme get you,' she said stiffly. 'I can't do this.'

He nodded briefly in the faint light and then bent over the cow.

'Hell,' he swore violently, his fingers feeling the taut, stretched flesh. 'She's as dry. . .'

'I've sent Graeme for hot water and soap,' Beth said briefly and he looked up at her.

'So we can save your half of a half-dead calf,' he said ruefully. 'Edgar told me. You push yourself past the limits of duty, don't you, Dr Sanderson?'

She winced at his tone. 'Someone has to,' she whispered.

'You seriously expect me to send you the bill for this?'

'I don't expect you to do anything,' Beth snapped. 'Except save this calf.'

Graeme Edgar returned moments later, parking his truck where the lights lit up the distressed animal. He emerged with arms weighted by two vast buckets. 'There's soap dissolving in the bottom,' he said briefly but Ewan had already found it. He had pulled off his coat and sweater, rolled up his sleeves and was now soaping his arms to the elbow. Beth grabbed the other cake of soap, placed a towel between the calf and the dirt and started soaping the back quarters of the calf. She knew what had to be done if there was any chance at all.

Then it was up to Ewan. He knelt, and gently, inexorably, forced the calf backwards. Back into the birth cavity. The cow's contractions seemed to have ceased but, even so, Ewan was working against massive forces. Beth soaped as he pushed, her small hands moving the slippery stuff over every surface.

And the calf moved. The legs disappeared, oh, so slowly, back the way they had come.

And then the real work began. Ewan's arms were in the uterus up to his elbows as he worked frantically to turn the small creature within. He had to get her round before the next contraction came. He had to. . .

The contraction came too soon. Beth saw the rippling of the muscles and called out a warning, but Ewan knew. He lay, his hands rigid, holding the calf in place with sheer brute strength while the contractions squeezed his arms until he swore savagely in pain. There was nothing Beth could do. She was running soapy water over the entrance to the uterus — over Ewan's elbows—but her action was all but useless. . . If Ewan couldn't turn the calf. . .

And then she saw the cow's swollen belly bulge and shift as her burden moved within. Ewan's body moved convulsively as his arms were caught. He swore again, his body lying flat against the ground and his arms disappearing into the cow. Then he gave a grunt of pure satisfaction and then another oath of pain. The cow's belly contracted strongly again and Ewan's arms shifted slightly.

Another contraction. The cow's eyes moved wildly, as if she knew this was her last chance. Her body gave a massive heave and the truck lights illuminating the scene showed a small black nose. And eyes. The ears were shoved ruthlessly out and the tiny head was clear. Ewan's hands were still somehow within and Beth knew they'd be bruised black and blue. Almost. . .

Another heave and the thing was done. A mass of body and blood and the beginnings of the afterbirth fell into Ewan's hands and the calf was born.

Ewan didn't stop. He lifted the calf clear, shifted the muck from its face and breathed strongly into the nose. The limp little bundle gave a tiny shudder and shifted slightly in his hands.

The exhausted cow stirred. Somehow she found the strength to turn her head. Ewan shifted the calf so its mother could reach. A long, rough tongue came out and licked.

'Well, I'll be,' Graeme Edgar breathed. 'It's a bloody miracle.'

'Yeah,' Ewan agreed wearily. 'Bloody is right!' He wiped his red-stained hands on a towel and looked with quiet satisfaction at mother and baby. 'A bloody miracle!'

'She's a ripper little calf,' Graeme said exultantly. 'To

survive that she'll survive anything. You've invested in a good 'un, Dr Beth.'

'It's just as well,' Beth smiled. 'We don't know what Dr Thomas will charge yet. He might charge like a wounded bull.'

'What will you charge?' Graeme said worriedly. They both looked at him and Ewan grinned.

'You needn't worry,' he told them. 'Once Dr Sanderson has deducted her fees for assisting and you, Graeme, have charged me for supply and cartage of hot water, there'll be precious little for me to stick on the bill.'

The cow stood up moments later, and Beth and Ewan helped load her and her precious calf on to Graeme's truck. 'She won't enjoy the jolting,' Ewan told them. 'But they'll be safer out of the weather tonight. Will you be right to unload?'

'Yeah.'

Beth looked closely at the farmer. There was something about him that she didn't like. The strain should have shifted but it was still in his voice. 'You can't do it alone,' she told him.

'The wife and Micky'll help me,' Graeme said. 'Do you pair want to come back for a wash and a cup of tea?'

Ewan shook his head and looked a question at Beth but she, too, thanked Graeme and declined. It would be easier to go back to her own home and clean up. 'Are you OK, though, Graeme?' The farmer was looking haggard.

'I'll be all right, girl,' he told her roughly. 'I could do with a good night's sleep. As I guess we all could.' He raised his hand in salute and left them.

Beth and Ewan stood watching as the little truck bumped carefully over the paddock and out of the gate. They walked slowly after, closing the gate behind them.

'You can go back to your beach now,' Beth said softly. She looked up at Ewan. 'Did you find any more penguins?'

The satisfaction in his eyes that had come with the birth of the calf disappeared and Beth cursed herself inwardly. He had almost forgotten.

'Three more dead ones,' he told her. 'With the lot this morning that's nearly twenty.' Ewan turned to stare bleakly out to sea. 'And that's only the one's we've found.'

'But. . . How much fuel did the yacht have on board?' Beth said slowly, her voice tinged with disbelief. 'I thought they only had a small auxiliary motor.'

'They did,' Ewan said savagely. 'Plus two drums of diesel fuel and a forty-four-gallon drum of sump oil. Sump oil. Thick and foul and deadly for anything swimming through it.'

'But why. . .'

'They were going to their holiday house down the coast. Bource tells us the house is miles from anywhere and has its own generator. Fuel is cheaper in the city than delivered by road in the country, so Bource decided to take the fuel by sea. He had the drums lashed on to the deck, but when the boat got into trouble they broke loose.' Ewan almost visibly ground his teeth. 'So he had diesel fuel and sump oil and no petrol to get himself out of trouble. He's got all the money in the world and less sense than a sparrow.'

Beth stood silent for a long moment, her gaze on Ewan's face. It was as if what had happened was physically hurting the man before her. He was exhausted and yet he was driving himself on — trying to escape something she couldn't begin to understand.

'Ewan, you need to rest,' she said gently. 'You don't need to look for any more birds. It's a tragedy, but

you've done all you can. And tonight. . .tonight wasn't
a tragedy.'

He glanced down at her but his eyes didn't see her.
'People don't think,' he said blankly. 'They just do what
they want and don't give a damn about the consequences. People. . .'

'Not all people.'

Ewan shook his head. 'I don't know where you fit in,
Dr Sanderson. With your blasted miracles. . .' He
turned his gaze across the coast-road and out to sea, a
lean, solitary figure in the dim moonlight. His solitude
was almost repelling. 'Stupid, stupid, stupid,' he said
and then shook his head as if warding off a bad dream.
'I was married once,' he said, in a different tone. It was
the sort of disinterested, flat tone one would use to
mention that it had rained last night.

'I know,' Beth whispered, wondering what was
coming.

'How did you know?' He hadn't turned but stayed
staring out to sea.

'I. . . It's common knowledge. Your television
career. . . Well, it made it public.'

'Yes.' He gave a short, harsh laugh. 'The public Dr
Ewan Thomas. Lucky Dr Thomas. Dr Thomas had
everything. Beautiful wife, lovely home, money. . .and
a child. Did you know he also had a child?'

Beth swallowed. There was something about the way
Ewan said 'had' that made her suddenly not want to
know more. 'No,' she said, with difficulty. 'I didn't
know that.'

'Not many people do,' he said, and Beth was aware
that he was almost talking to himself. It was as if the
memories welling up inside this solitary man were
suddenly too bitter to be contained. 'One of the few
things that Celia and I agreed on was keeping Sophie

out of the limelight.' He gave a harsh laugh. 'Though I think Celia only agreed because Sophie had a haemangiomia—a strawberry birthmark—on her face and it didn't look cute for the camera. The doctors were inconsiderate enough to say that birthmarks like that faded with time and it might scar if it was surgically removed. They refused to take it off—so Celia couldn't have all those lovely mother-daughter publicity shots she craved.'

'Ewan. . .' Beth cringed inwardly. 'Do you want to tell me this?' she asked gently.

He didn't hear her. Ewan was a long way away, and Beth knew that her company was simply a channel for catharsis. His bitter memories had to be released and she was here to provide that channel.

The doctor in her made her keep silent. She might not want to hear, but a silent listener was what this man needed, so a silent listener was what he must get.

'You and Celia broke up a year ago. . .' she said softly, letting him know that she was still beside him, and, despite her reluctance, ready to listen. The sleeve of her coat was brushing Ewan's thick sweater. She was intensely aware of his closeness, but Ewan stood alone.

'Celia and I broke up years ago,' he said. 'Emotionally if not physically. We should never have been married. She was. . .well, she was ambitious. I was a young, struggling vet and she believed in me—at least she seemed to. She was lovely, laughing—incredibly popular—and I didn't see until we were married that she was out for the main chance. Money and fame were all that mattered to our lovely Celia. We built up the television programme and at least we had that in common for a while. Then she fell pregnant and. . .and I at least hoped that it would work. Celia saw it as some glamorous, desirable thing to do. She had a vision of a gorgeous baby and heaps of publicity, and the reality of a disfigured daughter and two o'clock feeds didn't meet her expectations. She walked out on us when Sophie was three months old.'

'Oh, Ewan. . .'

'We were better off without her,' Ewan said harshly. 'I employed a housekeeper and kept on with the show. Much to Celia's chagrin the show went from strength to strength without her beautiful presence, and then — then the man Celia was with dumped her and people started looking at her as if she was a bad mother. There were whispers in the media about why Celia didn't have anything to do with her daughter. Celia had used what influence she had to keep Sophie's name from the Press but she was losing influence. So she decided that it was time she started playing the adoring mother again. She demanded access — not enough access to impede her lifestyle, you understand, but enough so she could play the devoted mother in front of people who mattered.'

He fell silent. Beth touched her lips with her tongue, tasting the salt of the sea-spray. 'So. . .so Celia has her now?' she said slowly.

'Sophie's dead.'

'Dead?' Beth's voice was a whisper, carried away by the sound of the sea.

'Dead.' Ewan turned to face her, his eyes looking straight through Beth's horrified gaze. 'Celia took our daughter — my little girl — to a Sunday lunch with some friends. There was. . .they were drinking. Sophie had just started to toddle about upright and Celia's friends had a swimming-pool. Do I have to say more?'

He didn't have to say more. The night spun before Beth and it was as if she saw this man for the first time. Worse, she saw the reason for the harsh and bitter mask. She saw a little girl, untended, toddling off toward a sunlit pool of water, while her mother. . . She closed her eyes. 'Oh, Ewan. . .'

He was totally silent. Beth fought for words but there was nothing. Finally, instinctively, in an age-old gesture of comfort, Beth put her hands up and clasped his head. She pulled his mouth down to hers and kissed him.

It was the first time Beth had done such a thing in her life. To kiss a man. . . The need to do so was unbearable, though. Beth was no longer in control and she knew it. Her whole being wanted to comfort this man and this was the only way—instinctively she knew that this was the only way she could do it. She pressed her body up against him and her lips held his. The wind blew around them—they stood unprotected on the deserted cliff-top road and she didn't care. Respond, her body pleaded. Respond. . .

For a long, long moment she didn't think he would. He stood, impassive and unyielding while her soft lips tasted his. Beth's hands dropped to his sides and found his fingers. She clasped them to her as if to impart warmth. Warmth and comfort. . . Warmth and comfort and love. . .

And then he broke. Like a drowning man clinging to a lifeline he moved, and his hands broke from hers to pull her tighter. Her body was lifted, pulled against his until the breath was crushed from her. She gave a thankful little cry that was lost somewhere in the lack of space between their mouths.

Drowning. . . It was an apt synonym. She was drowning in a crazy vortex of emotion that was so deep she felt she could never surface. Her mouth opened, wanting him, and his tongue came in to pierce the sweetness of her mouth. She welcomed him with joy, her breasts pressed hard against him.

Ewan, her heart was whispering over and over again

in an unspoken message of love. *Ewan. I can help you. I don't want you to hurt.*

And she knew that somehow, for this moment, she was driving away the worst of his demons. She knew that the emotion running between them excluded all else. She was no longer thinking of his wife, or his daughter, and as her tongue welcomed his — as her arms held him closer — she knew that neither was he. He was safe from pain in her arms. The kiss deepened and they were lost in each other.

Somehow. . .somehow the stiff material of Beth's anorak was no longer between them. They were standing on the leeward side of Ewan's truck, and with the warmth between them there was no need for a coat. It lay forgotten in a heap on the sandy ground. Ewan's hands were under the soft wool of her sweater, piercing the slit of her blouse, reaching to touch the tautness of her nipples.

Beth had never felt like this. Never. A fire was burning deep within her and she wanted him. She arched herself against him, a voice she didn't recognise moaning with desire as he bent to kiss the swelling buds at her breasts.

She was crazy. They were both crazy. The cold wind whistled around them but they were oblivious to its sting. Beth only knew she had to be closer to this man — closer than she had ever been in her life.

And then he was lifting her, holding her hard against him, his eyes staring down at her and she knew he was as desperate as she for what she was offering. 'Beth. . .' he said hoarsely, and she reached up to touch his lips with hers. He was bloodstained, bruised and battered from his fight for the calf and he was all the man she had ever wanted.

'I want you, Ewan,' she whispered and the old Beth,

the Beth of five minutes ago, wondered how she dared.
She smiled up at him, a wanton, wilful smile that told
him that she was much more sophisticated than she
was — that she knew just what she was doing. Now was
not the time to play the demure virgin. Not if she were
to comfort him. . . Not if she were to seduce him. . .

Seduce. . . The word came into her mind and it was
all she could do not to gasp. She had never thought that
she could act like this. Never! It wasn't Beth Sanderson
who was held in this man's arms, though. It was some
stranger — some woman she had never known until this
minute. She clasped her hands around his neck and
reached up to kiss him deeply on the mouth. This was
right. This was the only right thing in Ewan's tragic
world and it had to be right to give what she was
offering.

Ewan's hands were running down the curves of her
thighs, pulling her closer, making her body know his.
This man could do anything he wished with her. She
wouldn't fight him. She couldn't.

Slowly, he traced her lips with his fingers. 'Beth. . .'
The word was a caress. He looked down at her, his dark
eyes mirroring torment. Beth knew what it was. He
wanted her almost as much as she wanted him, but he
couldn't acknowledge it. To want a woman. . . To want
a woman was to let the world in again — expose himself
once more to the battery of hurt he was still suffering.
'Who are you?' he whispered. 'You're not human. A
sea-witch. An enchantress.'

She didn't answer but pulled him closer. Their lips
met again and they were melting into each other.
Becoming one, Beth thought hazily, and knew that, for
her at least, it was true.

'I'm yours, Ewan. For tonight. . . For tonight, take
the comfort I'm offering. Take me home and love me. I

want nothing in return. I'm asking nothing. I just. . .
For tonight, I just want you.'

Because I love you.

She didn't say the words but all of a sudden they were
there, ringing in her head as if they were suddenly the
only important thing in her life. She loved this man.
With her whole being, she loved him.

How long had she loved him? She knew. Beth could
trace her love to the moment on the beach that night of
the wreck, when he had cradled her to him and her
terror had somehow been absorbed by his strength.
Somehow, in that moment she had become one with this
man. He had saved her life and she belonged to him.
She belonged to him forever. She put her small hand
under his sweater, lifting the cotton of his shirt to feel
the tight muscles across his chest, her finger tracing a
path through the coarse hair. She was his and this was
her man. Now and for always. . .

'Not all women are like Celia,' she whispered. 'Not
all. . .'

His hands fell to run down the tight denim of her
jeans. 'I don't know,' he said hoarsely. 'Beth. . .' He
reached to let his lips kiss her tousled hair. 'You make
me feel as if there's a light at the end of a black tunnel.
But Beth, you're still at the end of that damned tunnel,
and I don't know whether I can go through. . .'

For answer Beth lifted her face mutely to be kissed.
Her eyes closed and her lips waited, waited. . .

He didn't kiss her. She wanted it so badly but in that
fraction of a second she felt him withdraw, and as she
opened her eyes, the radio attached to the belt at her
waist beeped furiously.

She could have wept. Beth felt like lifting the receiver
and flinging it as far as she could but even as she thought
it Ewan was rising. He had hesitated before the beeper

had sounded, Beth realised. He pushed her back to stand before him and for a moment Beth saw the flicker of something in his eyes that might have been relief.

'You're needed, Dr Sanderson.'

'Yes.' Beth let her breath go in an uncertain rush. Had there really been relief in his eyes? Had she imagined it? Her body felt as if it no longer belonged to her and desolation washed over her in a cold wave. The sheer impossibility — stupidity — of what she had tried to do washed over her like a cold shower. To make a man love her by throwing herself at him. . . She pushed back from his now loose hold and he released her.

'I. . . I'll have to go,' she whispered. 'They wouldn't contact me unless it was urgent.'

He stood silent.

'Goodnight then, Ewan,' she whispered bleakly.

He raised a hand as if to touch her but then let it fall back to his side. It seemed that there was nothing more to be said.

'Goodnight,' she whispered again and turned and fled.

As she ran back down the road towards her car she was aware of Ewan standing still on the windswept headland, staring after her.

CHAPTER SEVEN

THE ward light was on at the hospital. Beth saw it as she rounded the headland leading to the settlement and at the sight of it she put her foot on the accelerator. Whatever she had left — whatever emotional turmoil was whirling round inside her head — there was something more important that she had to concentrate on now. At this time of night Coral would not risk waking all her patients by turning the ward light to full unless it was to cope with some major emergency.

Lorna. It had to be Lorna. Beth thought through the possibilities as she ran from the car and by the time she burst through the ward door she had a fair idea what to expect.

Lorna was in deadly trouble. From the door Beth could hear the gasping, choking breaths. Coral was bending over the woman, holding on the oxygen mask and fighting to keep it in place as Lorna's weak hands fought, trying, panic-stricken, to remove it. The elderly patient was clearly terrified. Her breath was coming in shallow, whistling gasps and her body was convulsing with the frantic effort to get more air. And still she fought with Coral. It was as though she thought the oxygen was suffocating her. Coral looked up as Beth entered, her face reflecting sheer relief.

'She's getting worse,' she whispered fiercely as Beth approached the bed. 'Beth, do something. I think. . . I think we're going to lose her.'

Beth took a deep breath, catching at her professional self, forcing her mind to race through the possible causes of Lorna's distress. She seized the stethoscope from the bedside table and listened, her fingers on Lorna's pulse as she did. 'Blood pressure?' she snapped.

'I. . . I haven't taken it.'

'Then do it now. Leave the mask.'

'Leave. . . I've been turning the oxygen up full. She can't seem to get enough.'

'And she won't while she's in this state. Blood pressure, Sister, fast!' Beth's words were clipped and efficient, and they took effect. The middle-aged nurse snapped out of panic mode and into nursing efficiency, and within moments Beth had what she wanted. She nodded in satisfaction as Coral gave her the blood pressure reading, and her mind stopped its racing. The pressure was slightly raised, but for someone in Lorna's state of panic it wasn't unusually high. The nasty causes were fast being crossed off Beth's mental list to be replaced by something much more benign. This was something that didn't require medicine.

Turning from the night sister, Beth seized Lorna's hands and held them tight, sinking to sit on the edge of the bed. Lorna's breathing didn't ease. The awful whistling went on, but at least without the fight to rid herself of the mask there was less energy expended. Beth's hold on Lorna's hands grew tighter and she bent over the bed.

'Lorna, you have to stop this.'

Lorna's eyes widened. She stared up at Beth but she wasn't seeing her. Heaven knew what demons she was seeing. She arched her body again and Beth's voice sharpened.

'Lorna, you're panicking for no good reason. There is absolutely no reason for you to be doing this. I've checked. There's nothing wrong with you. I thought you must have a pneumothorax at the very least the way

you're acting but you've no such thing. You're fine. It's
only your fear that's making you breathless. Now, if you
can get a hold on yourself, I can help, but it's up to you.'

The night sister stared at Beth, shocked at her
unsympathetic tone, but Beth gave a small shake of her
head, silently bidding the nurse to remain silent. This
was no time for sympathy. Lorna's blind panic was
dangerous in itself. She gripped Lorna's hands even
tighter. 'Get a hold on yourself, Lorna,' she snapped.
'Now. Let Coral put the mask back on so we can
increase your oxygen levels, but start breathing normally. Slowly! Now, Lorna!'

Lorna's eyes somehow found Beth's. The pupils were
dilated with terror but somehow they focused and held
Beth's gaze. Beth took a deep breath. She had Lorna's
attention and the battle was almost won.

'I want you to breathe as normally as you can. Do you
hear? If you do what I say then you'll be fine. I promise.
Now breathe! And stop fighting. Will you let Sister put
the mask back in position?'

The terrified eyes stayed widened and Beth thought
what she was attempting wasn't going to work. The
silence stretched on and on and then suddenly Lorna
gave an imperceptible nod. Her body went limp. Coral
slid the mask back over Lorna's nose.

'Great,' Beth murmured. 'Now, get that breathing
slower, Lorna. You can do it.' Beth found herself
relaxing and looked up to smile at Coral. 'No sweat,'
she smiled.

'What on earth. . .?' Coral was practically gaping at
her. 'You mean there's nothing wrong?'

'Nothing that reassurance won't cure.' She looked
back at Lorna. 'Better. . .?'

The woman gave a tiny nod. Lorna's breathing was
still laboured but not frantic or distressed.

'It was just a panic attack,' Beth told Lorna softly. 'What was happening to you has very little to do with your medical condition, although the anxiety from it probably triggered it off.' She smiled. 'You can talk yourself into believing you're dying if you try hard enough.' She lifted the mask momentarily.

'Oh, Beth. . .' Lorna looked up at her. 'Oh, I've caused so much trouble.'

'No.' Beth shook her head. 'I should have given you something to help you sleep,' she told her. 'I might have known you'd lie awake and work yourself into a fine old state of anxiety. Last night you were exhausted, so you slept. Tonight you weren't as tired so you lay awake and fretted yourself into panic. I'll give you some tranquillisers to get you through the rest of the night, but I'm sure you'll be OK now. When was the last time you left Fergus alone?'

'We've never been parted,' Lorna whispered. 'In forty-six years of marriage we've never had a night apart until last night. And now. . . Now he'll be on his own for ever.'

'Nonsense,' Beth told her. She was holding the mask just away from Lorna's face so that the woman could speak but was still breathing oxygen. 'You have some financial organisation to do but once we get that oxygen concentrator at home for you, you'll be fine.' She looked appraisingly into the woman's disbelieving eyes. 'Emphysema patients can live for years and years — no kidding, Lorna — there are people whose condition is as serious as yours who were at home with an oxygen concentrator when I was in my first year of training and who are still happily at home today. You sleep with the oxygen on and you put it on during the day after exertion, but otherwise you can be free and lead a really satisfactory life.' She smiled. 'It doesn't even have to interfere with your sex life.'

Lorna looked up at Beth, her face torn between desire and disbelief. 'Even if what you're saying is true,' she whispered, 'where would we get the money? An oxygen concentrator costs thousands.'

'We'll find a way somehow,' Beth promised, her voice more sure than she really felt. Unasked, Coral had brought tablets and Beth proffered them, supporting the exhausted woman with her arm while she swallowed. 'That will make you sleep,' she promised. 'I hope Fergus is sleeping as well.'

'I hope so, too,' Lorna said wistfully, her voice slurred with exhaustion and tears.

'Well, if you're worried,' Beth grinned, 'maybe we'd better check on him.'

'I wish you would,' Lorna whispered.

Beth looked down at her. It was late and the elderly farmer needed his sleep but Lorna's fright was still almost tangible. She nodded. 'If you let Coral set your bed to rights and tuck you in for the night I'll phone him now,' she said.

To her surprise Fergus Mackervaney answered on the second ring. 'What is it?' he gasped, before Beth could say a word. 'Not Lorna?'

Beth smiled into the phone. 'Lorna's fine,' she said swiftly. 'But she's lying awake fretting about you, so I thought I'd better ring and make sure you're behaving yourself.' She smiled wickedly over at Lorna and raised her voice so Lorna could hear. 'You're not entertaining wild women or sleeping with your boots on, are you, Fergus Mackervaney?'

The elderly farmer chuckled in delight and Beth knew that it had been the right thing to do to telephone. He'd been as wakeful as his wife. 'Tell Lorna to get off my back,' he snorted. 'Can't a man have one orgy in forty-six years?'

Beth shook her head and smiled across at Lorna. 'We're interrupting all sorts of wild goings on,' she told her. And then she picked up the telephone and carried it across to the bed. Lifting the oxygen mask, she handed the receiver to Lorna. 'Put the nasal inserts back in,' she told Coral. 'I think Lorna will be fine with them now. Say goodnight to your husband, Lorna, so he can get back to enjoying himself.' She turned away.

In the next bed Robyn Bource was wide awake, staring across the room. Beth flicked the main switch so that only the dim floor-lights illuminated the scene once more and crossed to Robyn.

'I'm sorry you were disturbed.'

Robyn shook her head. 'Don't apologise,' she faltered. 'I thought. . . I thought she was going to die.'

'So did she,' Beth told her. She straightened the young woman's covers. 'The mind can do dreadful things.' She hesitated. 'Stress can do a great deal of damage,' she said softly. 'For instance, it can make you more tired than running a marathon.'

'Is that why you're keeping me here?' Robyn said wonderingly. 'Is that why I'm so tired?'

'I think it's part of the reason.' Beth met her look. 'Maybe things aren't quite as good as you'd like them to be between you and your husband. Am I right?'

Robyn's soft blue eyes filled with tears. With her long blonde hair splayed out across the pillow she looked absurdly young to be a mother — and very vulnerable. 'Forty-six years, Lorna and her husband have been married,' she whispered. 'And John and I have hardly had one year together. But I can't. . . I can't make it work.'

'You can't,' Beth told her, touching her tear-stained

face gently with one finger. 'Not on your own, you can't. It takes two to make a marriage work and I've a feeling that your husband has some growing up to do.'

Ten minutes later the clinic was quiet once more. Lorna had drifted back into sleep. Robyn Bource was staring wakefully into the dark but there was little Beth could do about that — and, in fact, it would probably not harm her to spend some quiet time thinking things through. The young woman was coming to terms with a few unpalatable facts and there was hardly an easy way for that to happen. Beth left her to it, walking out into the foyer with Coral.

'They should be right now,' she said quietly. 'I'll go back to bed.'

'Mmm.' Coral looked appraisingly over at Beth's strained eyes. 'You look as if you need your bed almost as much as this lot do. Were you out on a call when I tried to phone you?'

'Yes.' The word slipped out fast — too fast — and Beth blushed crimson. She turned away so that Coral didn't see, but little escaped that lady's kindly eyes.

'Well, you're going home to bed now, though, aren't you, Doctor?' There was no mistaking the firm warning behind the words and Beth almost smiled. Coral wouldn't gossip, but she could certainly let her disapproval be known.

'Yes, ma'am,' Beth said meekly and Coral grinned at her.

'Get on with you, Dr Beth,' she smiled. 'Bed!'

Beth walked slowly outside. She felt as if someone else rather than Beth Sanderson was standing there. The wind was freezing on her face and she welcomed its icy blast. She wanted something to wake her up from this strange, dreamlike evening. Too much had happened too fast. She walked a couple of steps further and

Ewan stood up from where he had been sitting on the stone fence. In his hands he held the anorak she had abandoned in her haste to leave him.

'Just returning your discarded clothing,' he told her drily. 'How are you at treating piles? These stones are freezing.'

Ewan smiled, but his smile was not that of a lover. His eyes were distant, as though he were appeasing a child and thinking of something else while he was doing it.

'You could have left it on my porch. Or come into the clinic if you were mad enough to wait,' Beth faltered.

He came closer and took her hands in a gesture of comfort. 'That would have been crazy,' he said gravely. 'The islanders would have had us married by morning.'

'Fate worse than death,' Beth whispered, trying to disengage herself and failing.

'I'll not go down that road again in a hurry,' he agreed. He let her pull back from him but kept his grip on her hands, holding her firmly at arm's length. 'Beth, love. . .'

'I'm not,' she said quickly, averting her face from his. 'Don't call me that.'

He drew in his breath. 'Beth. . .'

'Let me go,' she whispered. 'Please, Ewan.'

His hands gripped tighter. 'You're crying!'

'I'm not.' Beth pulled her hand from his and dashed it angrily across her wet cheeks.

'Beth, are you imagining you're in love with me? Is that why. . .?'

'Of course it's not,' she managed. 'I make love to anyone who wants me. I'm the island whore—didn't you know?'

'The islanders say you haven't had a boyfriend since you arrived.'

'So, no one wants me.' She shoved back from him,

fighting his hold. 'And it's no business of theirs—or yours either. Ewan, let me go. Please. . .'

'You kissed me—you let me kiss you because you felt sorry for me?' He seemed almost to be searching for reassurance.

'What other possible explanation could there be?' Beth spat at him. With a last angry wrench Beth was free. 'I feel sorry for you because you're more lonely than me, Ewan Thomas, and a damned sight more bitter. And I was lonely too but you've made me feel more alone than I've ever felt in my life before, and a darned sight cheaper.' She gasped on a harsh, choking laugh. 'So how can what I'm feeling be love? You tell me there's no such thing and you should know, world-weary as you are. How can I love you? You don't want me, do you? You kissed me because you were trying to forget. You were using me, Ewan Thomas, and I'm starting to feel used.'

The silence between them stretched on and on. In the distance, the sea crashed over and over on the shore and somewhere a sandpiper piped plaintively for morning. Beth stood motionless, her body cold and rigid, bracing herself for what was to come. She had asked for it. She had exposed herself to a pain she had never thought it was possible to feel.

'I suppose I was,' Ewan said at last, his voice blank and lifeless. He touched her face lightly with a finger. 'Beth, I was a bastard to let that happen. God knows, I don't want to hurt anyone—least of all you.' He took a deep breath. 'You can't love me, Beth. Loving me is like loving an empty shell. I've no more love to give.'

'You still love your wife?' The question was out before Beth knew she was going to ask it, and it hung between them like a vicious, spiked shield.

'No,' Ewan said flatly. 'I don't love Celia. I told you, Beth. I don't love.'

Beth nodded mutely. Tears were still running down her face. She looked up at Ewan and her heart wrenched within her. Slowly, she took his cold hands in hers, raised herself on her toes and kissed him gently on the lips.

'I'm sorry, Ewan,' she whispered. 'I'm really sorry.' She grabbed her anorak and fled.

Beth didn't see Ewan for the next three days. It was just as well, as her rigid self-control threatened to break at any minute.

You're behaving like a moon-struck teenager, she chastised herself but her scolding did no good at all. If only I hadn't let him touch me, she groaned for the umpteenth time. If I didn't know how good it could be. . .

You know how good it would be before he ever kissed you, she responded truthfully. You knew the moment you set eyes on him, even before you knew there was a reason for his surliness.

Men, she thought savagely as she slammed her kettle on the stove. They cause more trouble than they're worth. Her last consultation for the day had been with an unrepentant John Bource and she was still fuming. A local fisherman had decided to make a dash for the mainland with a haul of crayfish caught before the bad weather set in, and Bource had talked him into offering him and his family passage back to Melbourne. He'd come to tell Beth that he would be taking Robyn and the baby from the hospital at dawn the next morning.

'You can't,' Beth had said blankly. She had stared, astounded at John Bource's urbanely smiling face. 'You realise that Pete Inne has the reputation for being the

craziest fisherman in these parts. He takes risks the
other fishermen think are suicidal. He's the only one
here who'd be mad enough to take a boat out in this
weather.'

'That's why we're going with him.' John Bource had
spread his hands. 'Look, it's not through choice. If there
was any other way to get off this God-forsaken island
I'd take it, but there's not. I can't get a charter vessel or
a flight and every day spent away from my business is
costing me money. We were going down to our holiday
house for a couple of days — not two weeks!'

'And you'd risk your family's lives again rather than
cost yourself money?'

Bource's eyes shifted away from Beth's cold gaze.
'It's not a risk,' he had muttered. 'Inne tells me —— '

'Pete Inne will tell you anything if he thinks he can
make money,' Beth had snapped. 'He's made from the
same mould as you. Don't tell me he's not charging you
exorbitant rates to take you because I won't believe it.'

'The man's got a right to charge a fair rate,' John
Bource had said.

'You can do what you like, of course,' Beth had said
through clenched teeth. 'I can't stop you. But I'll tell
Robyn what I've told you, and privately I'll tell you to
your face that you're a damned fool. You've been
incredibly lucky once and your experience has taught
you nothing at all. I'm starting to think I would have
done Robyn and Sam a favour if I'd rescued them and
then cut the rope!'

Afterwards, she couldn't believe she'd been so blunt.
The Beth of a week ago could never have been so
forthright, but Robyn Bource was hurting as much as
Beth and for less reason.

A knock on the door shook her out of her reverie,
and Beth glanced at the clock on the wall. It was eight at

night. Too late for callers—unless she was wanted by one of the islanders who didn't have the phone connected. She rose to answer it, half welcoming the interruption to her bleak thoughts.

It was Micky Edgar. He stood on her back door step, hopping from one foot to the other in excitement.

'Doc, come quick,' he stammered. 'Doc Thomas is going to let your penguin go, and he says we can watch if we want.'

Beth smiled down at the excited little boy. Micky was suffering an extreme case of hero worship, she diagnosed. The child was wearing scruffy jeans and his sweater bulged with an indeterminate lump. While she watched, the lump gave a decided wriggle.

'That's not Buster?' she smiled.

'Course it is,' Micky told her. He lifted the sweater and the little dog's eyes peered out. They showed a definite sparkle. The disreputable little animal wriggled his tail in an ecstatic greeting, letting his master know in no uncertain terms that he would like to be put down so he could carry this greeting out in a more appropriate manner.

'You can't get down,' Micky said severely. He looked up at Beth, one medical expert discussing a case with another. 'The wound's still sus. . .susceptible to damage,' he told her seriously. 'Buster could bust his stitches—or make the dressing dirty so he'll get an infection.'

'You don't think he'd be better lying quietly at home?' Beth ventured and Micky shook his head firmly.

'He worries about me,' he explained. 'And he keeps trying to get to the back door to see where I've gone. So it's best if I carry him. But anyway, Dr Beth, you gotta come. You do want to see the penguin let go?'

'Is she better?' Beth asked.

'All better.' Micky nodded importantly. 'I've been helping Doc Thomas feed her. Because today's Saturday, Doc Thomas let me spend the whole day with him. This morning we filled the bath with sea water and gave her a test swim. She's totally waterproof again,' he ended triumphantly.

'Oh, Micky, that's great.'

'So come and see her off,' Micky pleaded. 'After all, it was you who rescued her. She probably wants to say goodbye,' he added.

'A penguin!'

'She's smart,' Micky said indignantly. 'She knows we've been helping her. She doesn't even try to bite — at least,' he added honestly, 'not very hard.'

'Well, I'm glad she's better,' Beth smiled. 'But. . . But it's late, Micky, and I'm tired.'

'Doc Thomas says we can only release her after dark,' Micky explained. 'He says she'll be less confused that way.' He looked pleadingly up at her. 'And you really ought to come,' he told her. 'You found her. You should let her go.'

Beth nodded slowly. If all she had to do was to carry the penguin down to the beach then it wouldn't take her long. She would see Ewan but she could escape quickly — and it would be good to see her little penguin swim free. One light in a bleak day. . .

'OK, Micky,' she agreed. 'I'll get my coat.'

Ewan was waiting for them outside as Beth and Micky walked over to his cottage. The sight of him standing there made Beth feel strange, but it was something she was going to have to accustom herself to. She couldn't live in a restricted environment like Illilawa and avoid seeing him. Ewan looked up from where he was standing at the back of his four wheel drive and smiled at

Micky as they approached. His gaze carefully avoided Beth.

'Success, Micky? I didn't think you'd talk Dr Beth into such a thing.'

'I'd like. . . I'd like to see the penguin once more before she's released,' Beth said stiffly. She looked doubtfully into the back of Ewan's Land Rover. There was a crate there which looked very much as if it could house a small penguin. 'Aren't you just taking her down to the beach?'

'No,' Ewan told her, his voice formal. He carefully closed the doors of the Land Rover without slamming them. 'We'll take her out to the rookery. She'll be confused enough without letting her go where she has to find her way home. This way she'll have all night in the rookery getting used to the feel of being back before she's tempted to go near the water.'

'I see.' Beth's tone was non-committal, carefully disguising the dismay she was feeling. How to avoid going now — with both Ewan and Micky clearly waiting for her to get into the Land Rover? Micky was already holding the passenger side door open for her, trying to hurry things along with an uncharacteristic display of social niceties.

'Come on, Dr Beth,' he hurried her. 'I haven't seen the penguin rookery for ages.' He grinned. 'I can't go there when Buster's well, because he's not very well-behaved,' he admitted.

'Why don't I stay here and look after Buster now?' Beth said feebly. 'I. . . He might get away and scare the penguins.'

'I've got him tight,' Micky informed her. He held the door wider and jiggled impatiently. 'Come on, Dr Beth. Dad says I gotta be home by nine o'clock and it's eight already.'

Beth cast a faltering look up at Ewan but he was ignoring proceedings. He had walked to the other side of the truck to climb into the driver's seat. Clearly he wasn't affected in the least by her emotion. Beth winced inwardly and then climbed in to the seat beside him. There seemed nothing else for it.

Ewan hardly spoke on the way out to the rookery and neither did Beth. They didn't have to. Micky kept up a stream of cheerful chatter from the back seat.

'The penguin's recovered really well,' he informed Beth knowledgeably. 'Some birds take weeks and lots don't get better at all. Dr Thomas thinks it's because she's so young. Isn't that right, Dr Thomas?' And then before Ewan could agree or disagree he went on. 'It's really lucky she's so young. If it had been next season she would have had eggs or chicks.'

'As would most of the penguins that died,' Ewan interspersed grimly. 'Luckily, it's near the end of the breeding season.'

Beth nodded silently. The presence of the big man beside her was doing strange things to her breathing. She felt a little like Lorna Mackervaney — as if she was lacking lung capacity. Only Beth didn't have a heart condition as well. . .

Finally, Ewan pulled off the road near the sheltered cove where the penguins' rookery had been since time immemorial. It was close to the southernmost tip of the island — as far away from the settlement as it was possible to be without a boat. Beth climbed from the car and looked about her. It was the mildest night they had experienced since the night of the wreck.

'That's why I'm releasing the penguin tonight,' Ewan told her when she commented. 'The forecast is for dirty weather again by tomorrow afternoon and I want the bird to be acclimatised to the sea before then. Ideally,

I'd like to keep her another twenty-four hours but birds develop all sorts of complications in captivity — pressure sores on their feet, for instance — and if it blows for a week she'll start developing them.'

Beth nodded. Ewan was clinically professional and she intended to be the same. Politely aloof. . .

Micky was already clambering over the rocks towards the rookery. He looked back impatiently. Beth could see by his stance that he was aching for them to follow but Ewan had clearly warned him about making too much noise. He stood, jiggling in small boy fashion, while Ewan lifted the crate from the back of the Land Rover and followed.

Despite the underlying tensions it was a lovely little ceremony. The three humans stood at the tip of the rookery, disturbing the few birds on the outer edge but making no noticeable impact on the bulk of the birds. The stench was appalling. Beth stood with her nose wrinkled, trying to ignore the odour of layer upon layer of guano. Then Ewan set the crate down on a smooth slab of granite and opened the cage door. The smell forgotten, Beth held her breath and waited.

The little penguin walked a few uncertain steps forward into the moonlit night. Then she stopped, uncertain. It was almost as though she couldn't believe her luck. Her beady eyes gazed around, taking in the moonlit picture before her. She looked and looked. She fluffed her feathers and looked again. Then, with quiet dignity, she turned back to stare for a long moment at the humans who had released her.

It was a moment of sheer, poignant beauty and Beth suddenly blessed Micky for making her come. Despite her discomfort in being with Ewan, this moment was worth it. She gazed down at the little bird, her breath caught in her throat. This one at least had survived the tragedy.

The moment was over. With one final, sweeping glance, the little bird turned away and moved forward into the sea of black and white feathers. In less than a minute Beth couldn't tell the bird apart from the others in the dusk.

'You're crying,' Micky said suddenly, staring up at Beth. He sighed at Ewan, man to man. 'Why do girls always cry for the stupidest reasons?'

'Their reasons aren't always stupid,' Ewan said softly, and both Beth and Micky had to strain to hear above the squawk of the penguins and the surf beyond. Ewan looked up at Beth as she flushed and averted her tear-stained face. 'Sometimes they cry for the best of reasons. Didn't you feel a bit choked up, Micky?'

'Sort of,' Micky said carefully, giving little away. 'But you wouldn't cry, would you, Dr Thomas?'

'No,' Ewan said bleakly. 'But it might be better if I did.'

CHAPTER EIGHT

THEY drove home slowly. Micky sat in the back again, unusually quiet. 'Buster's tired,' he told them seriously. 'He needs to sleep.'

So do I, Beth thought bleakly, though she knew it was not lack of sleep that was making her so weary. She cast a covert glance at the man beside her. His face was set and grim — a man carrying the weight of the world on his shoulders. If only she could make him laugh. There seemed little likelihood of him ever doing such a thing.

They dropped Micky off outside his house and drove on in silence. The silence stretched out painfully but Beth couldn't think of a thing to say and Ewan seemed to be content with his own company. Content? No, Beth decided. Content was the wrong word. Resigned. Or imprisoned. As the image of prison sprang into her mind Beth explored it and accepted it as the truth. Ewan was haunted by the past and it was holding him back from any sort of future. And Beth? How much would she give to remove those bars he had around him? Did she have enough love — and was love enough?

Ewan slowed suddenly as if coming to a decision. He pulled over to the side of the road. Below them the moonlight stretched endlessly away to the Antarctic.

'Beth, I wanted to apologise,' he said softly, and Beth stared across at him.

'Apologise. . .'

'Beth, I'm feeling a damned criminal for making love to you. I should never have touched you.' He hesitated. 'I should never have let myself. . .'

It wanted only that. To make love to a man and have him apologise. . . Beth felt suddenly sick to the stomach. She looked blindly ahead, not trusting her voice to reply. There was nothing to say.

'You're a lovely woman, Beth,' Ewan said gently. 'And the last thing I want to do is to hurt you. What happened between us — well, it was madness. It won't happen again. It can't.'

'Why not?' Beth whispered. She was trembling and her voice didn't sound as if it belonged to her.

'Because I want no more relationships.' Ewan's hands clenched on the steering-wheel. 'I've been there, Beth, and I've seen what caring can do.'

'Does it make a difference if I. . .if I care for you?'

There was a long silence. Beth thought he wasn't going to answer. Then he reached forward and turned on the ignition again. 'No,' he said harshly. 'It can't.'

They were silent for the rest of the journey. Beth's fingers were clenching and reclenching with the sheer effort of being beside him. She wanted to stop — to get out and run — anything but sit beside Ewan as though they were strangers. Finally the lights of the settlement appeared and Beth closed her eyes in relief.

There was a truck parked beside Ewan's cottage and as they pulled to a halt Matt Hannah emerged from its cab. He raised his eyebrows in a teasing greeting to Beth. Beth flushed crimson at the farmer's obvious implication as Matt turned to Ewan.

'The island committee have been thinking of organising a welcome dinner for you, Doc,' he grinned. 'Though I see you're already being welcomed nicely by our Dr Beth. But seeing this weather's so bloody awful and hardly any of the fishing fleet's out, we thought we'd have it soon. Tomorrow night, in fact.'

'I don't want a welcome,' Ewan said bluntly.

'You don't get a choice,' Matt said bluntly. 'The president's working on his speech right now and the president's wife has baked three sponge-cakes already.'

'It might have been an idea to check with me first. . .'

'Yeah, well, we knew you'd be free.' Matt grinned again at Beth. 'Though I guess you might have a social engagement an' all.'

Ewan ignored the obvious implication, his eyes still distant. Then he glanced across at Beth. 'Compulsory?' he grimaced.

'I'm afraid it is,' Beth told him, pushing her discomfort aside as she sensed his real reluctance to have any such occasion forced on him. 'That is, if you don't want to offend half the islanders.' She shook her head. 'Or disappoint them. They'll be looking forward to a reason for a social outing.' The community was abuzz with the news of Ewan's arrival and if he refused to be welcomed the islanders would be hurt. Ewan shrugged.

'OK, Matt,' he said resignedly. 'Where do I go? The local hall?'

'Yeah. I'll come and collect you at seven tomorrow.'

Ewan shook his head. 'Dr Sanderson will know where to go. She can——'

Matt shook his head. 'Dr Sanderson will need her car in case she's called away.' His smile deepened. 'There's plenty of time for that later. . .'

Beth gasped. 'Matt. . .' she said weakly, but couldn't go on. She summoned a smile for the pair of them. 'Goodnight,' she said, and walked away with as much dignity as she could muster.

Sunday was always a quiet day and this one was no exception—in fact, somehow, it seemed quieter than usual. Again and again Beth found her eyes straying from what she was doing to the window through which she could see Ewan's cottage. 'Like a stupid child,' she told herself over and over but it did no good at all. Work was the only way she could take her mind off Ewan, and on Sunday there wasn't enough of it.

To Beth's relief, when she made her way over to the clinic Robyn Bource was still in bed and intent on staying. She was big-eyed and tearful, hugging her baby as if her life depended on it.

'John's so angry,' she said bleakly. 'I don't think anyone's ever talked to him like you did, Dr Beth.' She smiled wanly. 'And when I said I agreed with you. . .' She shrugged her shoulders. 'He lost his temper. I don't think. . . I don't think our marriage will last.'

'Would it have lasted longer if those things hadn't been said?' Beth said brutally. 'Robyn, there are forms of abuse just as terrible as physical abuse, but they don't leave physical marks. If you don't learn to stand up for yourself, you and your baby are going to be doormats for the rest of your lives. Is that what you want?'

'N. . . No.' Robyn Bource gave a hiccuppy sob. 'But I still love him.'

'And maybe he loves you,' Beth said gently. 'But if he does then it's time he started acting as if he does. He nearly drowned the pair of you with his stupidity. I can't believe he's willing to risk your lives again.'

Beth sighed to herself as she left the clinic, considering Robyn Bource's problems. Robyn was moving around the hospital building and going for short walks on the beach but was making no move to join her husband at the guest-house. Hospital, for Robyn Bource, was a refuge. It was just fortunate that her bed wasn't needed so Beth could grant her some respite.

In fact, she welcomed Robyn Bource's presence. Robyn's misery was keeping Lorna Mackervaney from dwelling too much on her troubles. For the fiftieth time

Beth went over and over her available sources of
funding in her head, trying to work out some way of
stretching funds to cover the cost of an oxygen concentrator so Lorna could go home. There just wasn't any.

Some days it all seemed too hard, she thought
bleakly, knowing that how she was feeling about Ewan
was permeating her attitude to her job. Normally, she
was accepting of the fact that half her job seemed to be
social work. Today. . . Well, if she had one more
patient in tears then she'd probably join them!

It was a stupid thing to think. No sooner than the
thought entered her mind than such a patient appeared,
and it wasn't just tears Beth had to cope with. She could
hear hysterical sobbing before the car pulled up outside
the clinic.

Beth groaned inwardly when she saw who it was.
Belinda Evans was nine years old, the indulged child of
elderly parents. Ross and Marge Evans had resigned
themselves to childlessness when Belinda arrived and
they could subsequently refuse her nothing. In conse-
quence, Belinda was a spoilt brat, who Beth saw about
once a week as her overanxious mother brought her in
for every tiny symptom to be checked. As Marge Evans
seemed to restrict her reading to medical encyclo-
paedias, the symptoms she found were truly amazing.

Now, though. . . Now there really was something
wrong. The normally staid Ross Evans was driving his
car too fast. The car pulled off the road in a spray of
mud and Belinda's screams issued forth. The middle-
aged farmer leapt from the car and grabbed Beth's arm
as she approached.

'Thank God you're here, Doc,' he said hoarsely.
'Belinda's had an accident.'

Beth was already reaching to open the back car-door.
From the screams uttering from the back seat she

expected murder and mayhem to be happening as Ross spoke. The child couldn't be dreadfully injured, she thought grimly—not if she were making that much noise!

She wasn't, but Belinda was in trouble for all that. The child held her hand out before her and her big brown eyes were wide with horror. From her hand hung a length of fishing-line, and Beth didn't have to unclasp the tightly curled fingers to know what she would find.

'Oh, dear,' she said faintly. Her heart sank. Belinda of all children! Fish-hook accidents were common on the island as most of the children here fished. Most children could be reasoned with, though, making hook removal a simple procedure.

'Show me your hand, Belinda,' Beth said gently. The child was still in the car, her face buried in her mother's breast. 'Do you have a fish-hook stuck under the skin?'

The child didn't stop screaming. She was beyond hearing, Beth thought.

'She has,' Ross Evans said tremulously. 'It's. . . It's awful deep, Doc. Will you. . . Will you have to cut it out?'

It seemed Belinda wasn't beyond hearing. Beth had thought the child couldn't scream any louder but here too she was wrong. The screams escalated to blood-curdling wails. Beth sighed and motioned to Belinda's mother. 'Bring her into the surgery.'

The child's screams changed tempo. 'I won't,' she screamed. She clenched her fists and pummelled her mother, and then screamed again as the injured hand hurt. 'I won't. I won't. Take me home!'

'Bring her into the surgery,' Beth said again over the screams and then winced as one of the child's flailing feet caught her squarely in the thigh. 'Belinda, you must stop this fuss. I'm not going to cut the hook out. What I do won't hurt. You'll be able to go straight back fishing.'

'Just be a big brave girl,' Mrs Evans wept tremulously. 'Come on, Belinda, darling. You must be brave!'

It was the last thing Belinda needed to be told.

'Come on, pet,' Ross Evans coaxed. 'We won't let the doctor hurt you.'

'Just bring Belinda into the surgery,' Beth said through gritted teeth. Her task was getting harder with every moment the child's parents sympathised. Belinda was going to have to be held down while she pulled the hook through and out, and Beth was starting to have grave doubts as to whether anyone could manage it. Certainly, Mr and Mrs Evans couldn't. Beth could call on Enid but Belinda was big for her age and stubbornly strong.

It seemed crazy to be forced into giving a general anaesthetic for such a small procedure. Beth caught a fleeting glimpse of Belinda's hand as the child swiped at her and her heart sank. It was a large hook and, by the look of it, deeply embedded.

It took the three of them to get the child into the surgery and by the time they were there Beth knew that the parents were worse than useless. Their presence simply goaded Belinda to fresh hysterics. Belinda clung to her mother as though she was all that stood between the child and death.

'Could you ask Enid to come over from the surgery,' Beth asked Belinda's father quietly, her voice hardly audible above the screams. If she could get rid of one of them. . .

Ross Evans looked reluctantly at his daughter and then shook his head. 'You'll have to ask her yourself,' he said bluntly. 'We promised Belinda we wouldn't leave her, and we won't break that promise, will we, Mother?'

Beth strove for patience. 'Mr Evans, it's hardly necessary. There really isn't any reason for such drama.'

'If our child has to be operated on then we'll stand by her,' the farmer said grimly. 'It was our fault. We shouldn't have let her go fishing.' He placed a hand on his daughter's head and a tear trickled down his cheek. 'Eh, I'm sorry, love.'

Beth was going to have all three of them in tears in a moment. She took a deep breath and reached forward to take Belinda's hand. She hadn't had a clear look at the injury yet and Belinda had been here for ten minutes. As she did, Belinda reached forward with her good hand and gave her a stinging slap on the cheek. 'Get away from me,' the child screamed. 'Take me home. I don't want to stay here. I don't!'

'What on earth is going on here?'

The hard, male voice brought them all up short. Beth put her hand up to her stinging cheek and swung round. Ewan stood in the doorway, his cool eyes taking in the scene before him. The cool, authoritative tone made even Belinda pause for breath.

Ross Evans was the first to regain his voice. 'Belinda's. . . Belinda's had a dreadful accident, Dr Thomas,' he quavered. He turned around to face his daughter. 'She's. . .she's hurt her hand. . .' Her father's words reminded Belinda of the part she was playing. She opened her mouth and started screaming again.

Ewan ignored the screams and turned to Beth. 'What's going on, Dr Sanderson?' he asked brusquely. His eyes turned to rest appraisingly on the injured child.

'Belinda. . . Belinda has a fish-hook caught in her palm,' Beth managed. Her face was hurting almost as much as Belinda's hand. 'If she would just calm down. . .'

'Then I suggest that's what Belinda does.' Ewan sounded entirely uninterested. He turned to the farmer. 'The removal of a fish-hook is a simple procedure. I'll assist Dr Sanderson if she requires any help. Could you and your wife wait outside?'

'No.' The farmer drew a deep breath. 'We promised Belinda we'd stay, didn't we, Mother?'

Ewan raised his eyebrows. 'Are you suggesting Dr Sanderson and I can't be trusted with your daughter's treatment?'

'I. . .'

'If you won't accept our treatment then you'll need a referral to a surgeon,' Ewan went on ruthlessly. 'With this weather it may be days before you can take Belinda to the mainland. The wound will almost certainly become septic if the fish-hook stays there until then, but the choice is yours. If you're prepared to risk your daughter's hand. . .'

'But. . .'

'Choose,' Ewan went on relentlessly. He crossed to the door and opened it wide, waiting. 'Even if you do wait to see a surgeon, he may still insist that you wait outside,' he added.

Ross Evans looked helplessly over at his wife. 'But. . .' he said again helplessly. Belinda was still sobbing but slightly softer now as she listened to what was going on.

'If you wish us to do this, then please leave now,' Ewan said, looking pointedly at his watch. 'Dr Sanderson and I have other things to do this afternoon apart from this very minor procedure. Now, please.'

There was nothing for the Evans parents to do. Marge Evans lifted her daughter's clinging fingers from her neck and stood, silently weeping. Belinda was shocked into passivity. For once in her short life things weren't going her way. As her parents made their way to the door Belinda stood and made a desperate lunge after them. Ewan moved to block her path.

'Sit down, young lady,' he said sternly. 'You are behaving like a spoilt child. Having a sore hand is no excuse for hitting the doctor who is trying to treat you.'

'She's rotten. I hate her. . .'

'Belinda, if I hear one more peep from you I will turn you over and spank you.'

Belinda gave a watery gasp. 'You can't,' she managed, but her eyes were uncertain as she stared openmouthed up at Ewan. 'Doctors aren't allowed to hit people.'

'I'm a vet,' Ewan told her firmly. He picked the child up bodily and placed her on the examination couch. 'According to our professional code, vets are not permitted to spank cats, dogs, horses or budgerigars. Our code of ethics says nothing about spanking spoilt children.'

Belinda's tear-stained eyes widened. She was on her own now, without the support of her parents, and clearly felt she was on shaky ground. 'I'm not a spoilt child,' she whispered tearfully. 'It's just. . . It's just my hand hurts.'

'Then stop behaving like one so we can fix it,' Ewan told her bluntly. 'Open your palm.' He turned to Beth. 'Dr Sanderson, I'm in a hurry,' he told her. 'Will you please remove this dratted hook.'

Three minutes later the thing was done. In Ewan's grasp Belinda sat cowed and submissive, waiting for the agony to begin. Beth injected a little local anaesthetic, cut the eye from the hook with wire snips and pushed the hook through. The curve of the hook made it easy to

push the metal through until the wicked little barbs were
clear. Once they were outside the skin, the hook slipped
out easily. Beth nodded her relief as the thing came
clear. It was a new hook without rust, which meant
infection was less likely. She cleaned the entry and exit
areas with antiseptic and placed a piece of gauze over
the wound — not because it needed it, but she knew
Belinda would feel cheated without a bandage of some
sort.

'All done,' she said cheerfully. She held up the hook.
'Would you like to keep the hook for show and tell at
school?'

'No,' Belinda said belligerently and then looked up
suspiciously. 'You mean. . . You mean it's out?' It was
as if she had been robbed of something and Beth smiled
to herself. Belinda had obviously been meaning to
scream blue murder at the first pain.

'Yes.' She smiled gratefully up at Ewan. 'We can let
Mr and Mrs Evans in now.'

'It almost seems a shame,' Ewan said, and he
responded to the smile with one of his own. 'Well done,
Dr Sanderson.'

'A tricky piece of surgery,' Beth said drily and she
opened the door.

Belinda's parents almost fell into the room. Mrs
Evans seized her daughter and hugged her hard.
Belinda immediately began to cry again.

'It's fine,' Beth said over the noise. 'The hook was
clean and the wound looks good. There won't even be a
scar. The only time a fish-hook scars is when someone
tries to pull it out backwards.'

Ross Evans shuddered. 'Thank you, Doctor,' he said
dramatically. 'And you too, Dr Thomas. You've
been. . . You've been very good. Mother and I were so

looking forward to your welcome tonight. I'm sorry we won't be able to come now.'

'Why on earth not?' Ewan said blankly.

'Well, we'll be home with Belinda, of course,' Ross Evans told him. 'We'd planned to take her, but clearly she should go straight to bed.'

'Nonsense.' Ewan picked up a swab from the table and tossed it into the waste container. 'Belinda could go straight back to fishing if she wanted to.'

'But Belinda's delicate. . .'

'Belinda, how old are you?' Ewan demanded, cutting across the child's reproachful sobs. Belinda hiccuped and looked up.

'Nine,' she managed.

'Then I suggest you start acting it,' he told her. 'You don't really want your parents fussing over you as if you're a baby, do you?'

It was clear this view of proceedings hadn't occurred to Belinda before. She stared up at Ewan suspiciously.

'Will there be dancing tonight after dinner?' Ewan asked.

The child nodded non-committally.

'Well, then.' Ewan smiled down at her. 'Are you going to let some trifling little cut stop you dressing up and taking the floor with me tonight?'

The child gasped. 'You mean. . . You mean you want to dance with me?'

'I might,' Ewan said thoughtfully. 'Especially if I thought you were grown up enough to apologise for that appalling fuss.'

'I'm sorry,' Belinda whispered, awed by the prospect of dancing with Illilawa's only television celebrity.

'Not to me.' Ewan touched her cheek. 'You hit Dr Sanderson.'

'She hurt me.'

'No,' Ewan said harshly. 'Dr Sanderson helped you, Belinda, and you hurt her. Now a mature young lady would apologise. A child would sulk. What's it to be?'

Belinda's eyes widened. 'A mature young lady,' she whispered. The thought was obviously very appealing. She took a deep breath and turned to Beth. 'I'm. . . I'm very sorry I hurt you,' she said. 'I was. . . I was silly. And I'm sorry I screamed, too.'

Beth smiled down at the child. There was hope for Belinda yet, if only she could escape the confines of her parents' cloying adoration. 'All forgiven, Belinda,' she said gently.

'Are you coming tonight?' Belinda asked Beth.

'I don't. . . I don't think so. I'm busy. . .'

'Of course she's coming,' Ewan said bluntly. 'If she doesn't then I don't.'

Mrs Evans looked from one to the other, her inquisitive eyes taking in the flush of Beth's cheeks that had little to do with the treatment Belinda had meted out. 'Oh,' she sighed. 'Oh, that's lovely.'

'You didn't have to say that.'

'What?' The Evans family were disappearing down the track and Ewan and Beth were left alone. Ewan turned to Beth, his gaze once again cool and uninterested.

'You didn't have to say if I don't go, you won't,' Beth said crossly. 'Now it'll be all over the island that there's something between us.'

'And isn't there?'

'Oh, yes,' Beth snapped. 'There certainly is. You kissed me and then you apologised. I should be grateful that such a famous television personality could pay me such flattering attention.'

The words were out before she considered and as

soon as she said them she regretted them. She was
floundering well out of her depth here and she knew it.
The hurt she was feeling made her want to strike back —
but she didn't want to hurt Ewan. She didn't! She had
offered her love of her own volition and she hadn't
demanded any response. So why now did it hurt so
much when he looked at her with those distant eyes?

'Matt's collecting you,' she whispered, her eyes welling with unshed tears. 'It doesn't matter one bit whether
I go or not, and you know it. Thank you for your help,
Dr Thomas. Now, if you'll excuse me, I have work to
do.'

She wanted him to stop her. Desperately, Beth
wanted him to reach out and pull her back — refute the
angry words she had just said. He made no such move.
Beth walked slowly back over to the clinic, aware all the
time of his eyes watching her retreat.

Beth found Robyn sitting up in bed cuddling Sam and
staring sightlessly in front of her. She looked up as Beth
entered and managed a wan smile. 'Hi,' she whispered.

'Hi.' Beth summoned a smile she was far from feeling.

'Dr Beth, I've just been telling Mrs Bource that she
should be going to the dinner tonight,' Lorna
Mackervaney said roundly from the bed. Her kindly
eyes were looking troubled. 'Her husband's just been in
saying he's going whether she does or not.'

Beth nodded. Any sign of activity on the island would
be welcomed by John Bource. 'You could if you wanted
to,' she smiled at Robyn. 'Coral would be delighted to
look after Sam, and it would do you good to have a
night out.'

'But feeding. . .'

'We'll help you to express some milk before you go,

in case Sam gets desperate, and you can come back when he's due for a feed.'

Robyn shook her head helplessly. The young woman seemed in limbo. The shock of last week's near-drowning plus facing the realities of her marriage problems seemed to have left her limp and helpless. 'John wants me to go,' she said slowly. 'But I haven't anything to wear.'

'You and Dr Beth are the same size,' Lorna told her. 'You've been wearing her jeans and sweaters when you go out for walks. I bet you'd lend her something pretty, wouldn't you, Dr Beth?'

'Of course,' Beth promised.

'You're going?' Robyn asked.

'I don't think so.' Beth turned to the desk in the corner and started fiddling with a pile of paper-clips.

'Oh.' Robyn sighed. 'Then. . . Then I won't go, either,' she said decidedly.

'Why on earth not?' Lorna demanded.

'Do you think John would bring me home just because Sam needs a feed?' Robyn sighed sadly. 'He wouldn't. Not if he's been drinking and is enjoying himself.'

'But you'd still like to go?' Beth asked slowly.

'If I did. . . If John could see that we can still have fun. . .'

Beth nodded. She closed her eyes, feeling rather like a cornered rabbit. 'Very well, Mrs Bource. I'll take you to your ball.' She forced a bright smile on to her face and crossed to the crib. 'And we'll bring you home as soon as your Prince Charming here threatens to turn into a pumpkin.'

CHAPTER NINE

BETH spent the rest of the afternoon regretting her rash promise. She went through her wardrobe and took her one warm evening dress over to Robyn, only to have it rejected. It was tight-fitting, and Robyn's breasts were swollen with milk. 'I'm going to bust out all over,' Robyn giggled. 'Besides which, Dr Sanderson, you can't tell me that it's not your favourite dress. This powder blue would look smashing on you.'

Beth looked doubtfully at the dress. She had bought it before she had come to Illilawa—a spur-of-the-moment purchase inspired by a rather attractive surgical registrar. She'd regretted buying the dress five minutes into the date when Tony had launched into his favourite topic of conversation—himself—a subject he so enjoyed that he immersed himself in it all evening—and it had hung uselessly in her wardrobe ever since. The soft blue velvet made her seem different somehow—a Beth she wasn't at all sure she should allow to be seen. She had no intention of wearing it tonight, but now both Robyn and Lorna had seen it and they weren't interested in her excuses.

'You could lend Robyn that black skirt and red crêpe blouse you wore to the Trotters' wedding anniversary,' Lorna said, thinking back. She fingered the dress Robyn had reluctantly removed. 'But you have to wear this yourself, Beth.'

'I couldn't,' Beth told them. 'It's much too dressy.'

'Nonsense,' Lorna told her. She was clearly enjoying interfering in the proceedings. 'You didn't tell Mrs

138

Bource here it was too dressy. You wear it.' She sighed wistfully. 'What I'd give to go.'

'We could take the oxygen concentrator across,' Beth said doubtfully, but Lorna shook her head.

'You know it has to stay here,' she told Beth. 'If there was an emergency and a young thing died because I was using it then I'd never forgive myself. No. My Fergus is coming in to be beaten at Scrabble while you two are off gallivanting. The only thing I ask is that you wear that dress, Dr Beth. In that dress you'll knock our Dr Thomas off his feet, no matter how many rich and beautiful young city women he knows.'

Beth drew in her breath. 'I'm not. . . I'm not trying to knock anyone off their feet,' she managed.

'Ho!' Lorna said scornfully. She turned to Robyn. 'Next she'll be telling me she's not interested in our Dr Thomas and then I'd know she was a liar.'

Robyn grinned as Beth's face turned scarlet. 'I don't think she can,' she agreed with Lorna.

'Just as long as you wear that dress.' Lorna pulled herself high on her pillows and fixed Beth in a gimlet gaze. 'You come over and show me you in that dress before you go,' she told Beth roundly. 'Or. . .or. . .or I'll take up smoking!'

Beth held up her hands in mock surrender but her colour didn't fade. Was she that obvious?

Her doubts continued as she dressed. The Beth staring back at her from the mirror seemed an echo from a forgotten past — a time when Beth had a social life. It truly was a beautiful dress. It clung and swayed around her in soft folds, and its tight-cut bust accentuated her lovely figure. Beth's hair hung in tumbling curls around her shoulders and her big green eyes were huge in her white face. She hadn't been sleeping and it showed, Beth thought bleakly, but the effect was almost ethereal.

She cast one last doubtful look in the mirror and turned away. If she kept looking—if she kept looking she would never find the courage to leave the house.

Robyn, Lorna and Coral had no such doubts. The nurse was brushing Robyn's long hair as Beth appeared and Robyn was protesting half-heartedly.

'I can do it myself,' Robyn was saying. 'Honestly, Coral, you'd think I was sick.'

'You're still my patient,' Coral said darkly. She looked up as Beth appeared and pursed her lips in a silent whistle. 'Well! Will you look what the cat just brought in?'

Beth coloured self-consciously and smiled. She smoothed a hand down the soft folds of velvet. 'It's too dressed up,' she murmured. 'I look. . .'

'I've seen worse things than that crawl out of cheese,' Coral grinned. 'What do you reckon, Lorna? Our Dr Beth scrubs up OK, doesn't she?'

'Oh, my dear.' Lorna's eyes misted hazily. 'When your young man sees you like that. . .'

'He's not my young man!'

'Well, if he's not your young man after tonight then I wash my hands of him,' Lorna said bluntly. 'Eh, it makes me wish I was forty years younger. I had a dress just like that.'

'And she looked even prettier in it.' Unnoticed, Lorna's husband had entered carrying his Scrabble set. He crossed to Lorna's bed and kissed her, then beamed at Robyn and Beth. 'They're a sight for sore eyes,' he told Lorna. 'But they're not a patch on you.' He grinned at Beth. 'But that young fella of yours is in for a rare treat tonight.'

'Look, for the last time,' Beth expostulated. 'Dr Ewan Thomas is not my young man!'

'Get on with you!' Fergus said.

'They're so in love,' Robyn said sadly as they drove around the coast to the hall.

Beth glanced across at the pale woman beside her. She looked desperately worried. Caught up in her own emotions, Beth had been silent, but now she forced herself to speak.

'The Mackervaneys?' She smiled. 'Yes, they are.'

'Is Lorna going to get home?' Robyn asked bluntly.

Beth shook her head. 'Not for quite a while,' she said sadly. 'There's no funding for an oxygen concentrator so they're going to have to buy it themselves. The only way they could afford such an expense is to sell the farm, and that's going to take time.'

'But. . .but they love the farm.'

'Yes,' Beth said grimly. 'That's the hardest part. The irony is that buying the concentrator to get Lorna home is going to deprive her of the only home she's ever wanted.'

Robyn fell silent. Beth cast a look across at her, encouraged by her concern for Lorna. At least Robyn was now able to think past her own problems.

Which is more than I'm doing at the moment, she told herself harshly.

The dinner was well under way when Robyn and Beth entered. They'd left their arrival until late to enable Robyn to give her baby his scheduled feed. It was better this way, too, Beth thought. If she had to arrive, it was better to arrive when the hall was crowded and she could avoid Ewan in the crush.

John Bource was waiting for them and Beth sighed as

she saw him. The man was still angry and he had been drinking.

'What kept you?' he said darkly.

'I had to feed Sam —— ' Robyn started.

'Sam! Doesn't it matter that you've made me look a fool. . .?'

Beth left them to it. Their problems were their affair. All doctors seemed to do was pick up the pieces after people had torn their lives apart, she thought sadly.

'So, you've decided to grace the occasion with your presence after all!'

Beth swung round. There was no mistaking that voice. Ewan was standing by the door watching her. His eyes travelled over her slim form but his face was expressionless. If he thought her dress attractive he certainly wasn't going to admit it.

Beth didn't speak. She couldn't. Ewan was looking at her as if he hated her — as if she was the last person he wanted to see. Beth stared up at him. In his dark suit and crisp white shirt he looked impossibly handsome — impossibly alone. How could she love him so much when he didn't want her? She turned blindly away and headed for the other side of the crowded hall.

The occasion was as festive as the island people could make it. The tables were groaning with food — every cook on the island had taken this evening on as a personal challenge. Beth chose a slice of quiche and then wished she hadn't. She certainly didn't have the heart to eat it.

She made her way through the throng of people, making polite conversation as she went. She was never as lonely as on these occasions. On the dance-floor there were couples already clinging to each other, and a laughing, smiling crowd of youngsters having fun. Beth was no older than many of them but always she was on the outside. The farmers and the fishermen came and asked her to dance but they treated her differently — with respect. And I'm sick to death of respect, she thought savagely. I might be a doctor but I'm too young for respect.

Ewan was on the other side of the room and that was the way Beth intended it to stay. She couldn't be near him and keep the smile on her face. As he moved from one group to another so did she — seemingly at random but in fact in careful lines to avoid him.

Why did she have to be so aware of him? What was making her act like a love-sick teenager instead of the mature adult she was? She was furious with herself but was powerless to stop the way she was feeling.

A small hand grasped her skirt and Belinda Evans materialised at her side. Most of the island's children were present — a fact of life on Ililawa when a social function meant that there were never any adults left over to act as babysitters. Belinda was charmingly dressed in pink organdie with matching hair ribbons, and was sporting her best party manners.

'My hand hardly hurts,' she said proudly. 'Do you think. . .do you think Dr Thomas will consider me grown-up enough to dance with?'

Beth looked across to the dance-floor. Ewan was deep in conversation with one of the island's more attractive young ladies. They had danced once and now were standing to one side deep in conversation.

'Why don't you go and ask him?' Beth told the little girl. 'I'm sure he intends to.'

Belinda gulped nervously and the hand clutching Beth's dress tightened. 'You see, I'm not quite game,' she admitted. 'I was wondering whether. . .whether you could remind him.'

Beth sighed and then summoned up a smile. The hurt

went on and on. She should never have started this. To have kissed such a man. . . Her pain was like a raw and aching wound. 'Come on, then, Belinda,' she said, taking the child's uninjured hand in hers. 'A promise to dance is a serious obligation and I know Dr Thomas won't want to forget.'

'Ewan. . .' she said quietly, as together she and Belinda approached.

Ewan turned at the sound of Beth's voice. Beth led Belinda up to him, dredging up a smile.

'Belinda's free for this dance,' she smiled. 'Her programme's almost full, so unless you want to miss out I suggest you seize this opportunity.'

Ewan's eyes flicked hers, and his mouth curved into a smile. He looked down and Beth's heart knotted at the thought that this smile wasn't for her. 'Miss Evans,' he said formally. 'I tried to find you before but you were surrounded by young men. May I have the honour of this dance?'

The girl Ewan was with frowned her annoyance. 'You don't have to dance with the children, Ewan,' she said tightly, glaring at Beth. Clearly she thought it was a ruse to disengage Ewan from her. 'They're supposed to dance among themselves.'

'And so the children can,' Ewan responded politely. He tucked Belinda's arm in his and motioned her forward. 'But Miss Evans and I intend to dance with each other.'

They moved away. The music struck up again and they were lost in the throng of dancers. One of the young fishermen appeared and tapped Ewan's late partner on the shoulder and then Matt Hannah bore down on Beth.

'Will you dance, Dr Beth?' He smiled down at her and took her arm. Despite the upbeat tempo of the music the big farmer moved deliberately into the only dance he knew—a shuffling approximation of a waltz. Beth resigned herself to his kindness, suppressing an ache of jealousy at the laughing couples around them.

'OK, ladies and gentlemen. Now you're all on the floor, let's form a circle for the Pride of Erin.' The bandmaster was intent on mingling the dancers. Beth's dance with Matt was cut short as the demands of the dance led her from one partner to another.

Around and around they went. The popular melody played over and over as the dancers changed and Ewan moved closer and closer. Beth mentally braced herself as she realised what was now inevitable. She was being silly, she told herself roundly. After all, she only had to dance a few steps with Ewan and then they'd move on. He was the one after the next. He was next. And then. . . She moved forward, Ewan took her hand and the music stopped.

'Thank you, ladies and gentlemen. Let's stay with the partner you're with for a while. We'll give you a nice slow waltz to catch your breath before we let you sit down.'

And she was in Ewan's arms, drifting effortlessly around the floor while he held her hard against him.

'Look, you don't have to do this,' she murmured. 'We could. . . We could just sit down.'

'And have half the island saying I snubbed the local doctor?' Ewan said softly. The music slowed even more and his hands held her tighter. 'Why the hell did you have to wear that dress?'

'What's wrong with my dress?' Beth demanded.

'Nothing,' Ewan snapped. 'That's what's wrong. Have you any idea. . .' He broke off, his hands pulling her even closer with a fierceness that was almost savage. Beth could feel the muscles in his chest rippling under

her breast. The music caught them in its rhythm and
they might as well have been alone.

Beth felt the tension in her body slowly dissipate.
Surely this had to be right. Surely this love she was
feeling was returned — must be returned. Her breasts
moulded to his body and she felt as if they were one
person. There was no separation. Separation was
impossible — now, and forever.

The music went on forever. Beth's steps were guided
by Ewan but she hardly felt his guidance. She knew
where he was going. She knew him. She was one with
him.

It had to end. The music finally ceased and their feet
stilled. Ewan put her at arm's length and she looked up
at him with overbright, confused eyes.

'Ewan,' she whispered.

'God help me, Beth,' Ewan said in a savage undercur-
rent. 'I don't want this. Do you hear me. . .?'

Beth shook her head blindly. 'I don't understand.'
She closed her eyes in distress. 'I don't understand
what's happening to me. . .'

'Dr Thomas has to finish the dance with me because
he started out with me.' It was Belinda, anxiously
jiggling up and down and hoping for attention. 'It's
proper, isn't it, Dr Beth?'

Beth nodded, her eyes carefully averted from Ewan.
'Of course it is,' she said. Then she looked around to the
edge of the dance-floor as someone called her name.

'You're wanted on the phone, Dr Beth,' one of the
young farmers called. 'Looks like your party's over, I'm
afraid.'

Her party was over. It was Coral phoning from the
clinic. 'Mrs Edgar's just brought her husband in,' Coral
said. 'He's had bad stomach pains all afternoon and he's

looking pretty sick. I think you should see him,' she said.

Beth nodded and looked around. She had missed the Edgars from the gathering. Micky usually made his presence felt in no uncertain terms and Beth wouldn't have been surprised to see Buster present as well. All the Edgar family had been absent, though, which meant that Elizabeth Edgar must be worried. 'I'll be there as soon as I can,' she said.

Out on the floor Ewan and Belinda were still seriously dancing. Beth cast them a quick glance and went to find Robyn Bource. 'I have to go back to the clinic,' she told her. 'Do you want a lift?'

'Yes.' Robyn was big-eyed and pale. She cast a glance to where her husband was the centre of a rowdy bunch of fishermen. 'John won't even know I've gone.'

Beth knew she was in trouble two minutes after she walked back into the clinic. Graeme Edgar was lying curled on the examination couch clutching his stomach in agony. Beth thought back to the birth of the calf. Graeme had worried her then. . .

'He's got stomach ache,' his wife said unnecessarily.

Beth nodded. She picked up Graeme's wrist and took his pulse and then reached for the blood pressure cuff. Neither were reassuring.

'Have you had anything like this before?' Beth asked. She frowned down at Graeme but the farmer was in too much pain to respond.

'He's got a hernia,' his wife said helpfully. 'He's had it for years but lately it's been giving him hell and he hurt it more trying to get the calf out the other night. I've told him and told him to come and see you but he wouldn't listen. He reckoned you might put him in hospital and he couldn't spare the time from the farm.

And now. . .' Her voice broke off on a sob. 'And then
he went out and stacked wood this afternoon and
suddenly he just doubled over. He. . . He is going to be
OK, isn't he, doctor?'

'Let's find out what the matter is first, shall we?' Beth
said gently. Micky was behind his mother, his face
scared. 'Micky, can you take your mum out to the foyer
and make her a cup of tea? Use lots of sugar.'

'Sure.' Micky was clearly relieved to have a job to do
and Beth noticed that Buster had been left at home.
Micky clearly regarded the situation as serious.

Beth and Coral worked swiftly. Coral appeared a
flustered, middle-aged mum to those who knew her only
in domestic situations, but in an emergency her fluster
disappeared to nothing and she became calm and
unflappable. She was a terrific nurse, Beth thought
thankfully, as together they stripped off the farmer's
clothes.

As the farmer's clothes fell away they exposed what
Beth had most been afraid of. Her heart sank. A loop of
bowel protruded through the farmer's groin in a fist-
sized lump. It must be twisting to cause the sort of pain
Graeme was in.

She groaned inwardly. This could be a disaster. If she
couldn't manipulate the bowel back. . .

'Graeme, how long has the hernia been like this?' she
asked, trying to make the man focus on her words
through his pain. If it had only just come through then
she could wait and see if it settled enough for her to
manipulate.

'Three. . .four hours, I reckon,' Graeme groaned. 'I
went to bed to see if it'd help. Damned lump's getting
bigger.'

Three or four hours. . . If the bowel had been twisted
for that long then the lack of blood-supply may have

already irretrievably damaged it. Beth mentally went over the operation in her head. It'd be OK if she just had to repack the bowel—but if it had started to die and she needed to do a resection. . .

It was too wild a night to call for help. An RAAF Hercules was usually on call for emergencies but not in this weather. The plane would be lucky to find the island on a night like this, much less land. These things flashed through Beth's mind as she mechanically gave morphine and set up a drip. Graeme was starting to retch with the pain and Beth looked up to Coral.

'Telephone the hall,' she said quietly. 'Get Dr Thomas. Tell him I have to operate and I need an anaesthetist. I need him now.'

'But. . .' Coral's eyes widened. 'The man's a vet, Beth. You know what happened last time you tried to use a vet as anaesthetist. Have you considered?'

Beth nodded, her eyes motioning to the patient on the bed. Whatever qualms she was feeling mustn't be communicated to Graeme. 'Your hernia is strangulating,' she told him softly, taking his hand. 'I'm going to have to operate, Graeme. You'll be fine. Trust me.'

Graeme's pain-dulled eyes widened. 'You and the vet?' he managed.

'Me and the vet,' Beth smiled.

'Well, I reckon if the pair of you can fix Buster then you can fix me,' he said hoarsely. 'The whole island reckons you make a good team. Only, for God's sake, Doc, make it quick.'

'I will.' Beth took a deep breath, planning the next few moments. Maybe it would be better if she talked to Ewan. 'Prep Mr Edgar, Sister, please,' she said. 'I'll ring Dr Thomas and Enid. We're going to need all the help we can get. Let's move now, Sister. Quickly.'

Coral was already moving.

It took more than twenty rings before anyone finally answered the telephone at the hall and when they did Beth could hardly make herself heard above the noise of the party. Obviously, things had livened up since she left.

'Tell Dr Thomas he's needed,' she yelled into the phone to the male voice who answered. 'At the hospital.'

The man at the other end of the telephone finally got the message. 'You're not going to drag him away, Doc?' he demanded incredulously. 'He's the guest of honour.'

'I need him, Jim,' Beth said curtly. 'Fast.'

'OK, Doc, if you insist. I'll go drag him off the dance-floor.'

Two minutes later Ewan came on to the line. By the time that he did Beth was close to screaming. She was wasting so much time. . .

'What is it, Beth?' Ewan's tone was clipped and efficient and Beth could have wept with relief.

'I need an anaesthetist,' she told him. 'Can you do it?'

'What's up?'

Swiftly she told him. 'There's a chance the bowel's been cut off for so long that it may already be dead.'

'That'd mean resection. . .' There was a brief silence. 'Hell, Beth. Can you do a resection?'

Beth took a deep breath. 'There's a first time for everything,' she confessed. 'I'm. . . I'm sorry to spoil your night but. . .but I need you. Hurry, Ewan.'

'I'm on my way.'

CHAPTER TEN

BETH spoke briefly to Enid and then slipped into her office and grabbed a text. Five minutes' reading, she promised herself, her thoughts jumbling in panic. It had been two years since she'd seen this procedure. Could she remember?

Ewan found her in her office soon after. Beth heard his quick steps through the clinic foyer and her office door swung open. He looked at the huge textbook and gave a rueful grin.

'You know, if I was a patient and I found my doctor swotting her text minutes before my operation I'd take off like greased lightning,' he smiled. Beth shook her head. She was too worried to respond even to Ewan's smile.

'If he could take off, I'd be the first one pushing him out of the door,' she admitted.

'You really haven't done this before?'

'I've seen it done,' she said worriedly. 'I've assisted a couple of times.'

'Well, I've done it on horses.'

Beth looked up. Her eyes met Ewan's and his were suddenly warm and reassuring. Despite her worry Beth found herself giving a faint chuckle. 'We're a fine pair,' she smiled. She looked down at the text. 'I just hope to heaven I can remember.'

'You can always rely on me,' Ewan told her. 'Mind you, our patient might just find himself gelded.'

Beth walked out of her office still smiling, and the sight of her face was enough to reassure Mrs Edgar and

Micky. They smiled back — frightened smiles which would have faded considerably if they'd been able to hear their doctors' last conversation.

'Oh, Doctor,' Elizabeth Edgar gasped. 'I'm so worried.'

'I don't think you should be,' Beth managed, avoiding Ewan's eyes. 'Dr Thomas is even more familiar with this operation than I am.' Behind her Ewan made a tiny sound that could have been a cough. 'Mrs Edgar, why don't you go home?' Beth said gently, ignoring her anaesthetist. 'It will be an hour or more before Graeme's awake and you'll be more comfortable there.'

'I'd. . . I'd prefer to wait,' Mrs Edgar said tremulously and Beth nodded.

'Look after your Mum, then, won't you,' she told Micky. The little boy nodded and moved closer to the woman beside him. As the door closed behind them Beth wasn't sure who was comforting whom.

The theatre was immaculate. Beth looked around checking that her list of instructions had been carried out, and then turned to the anaesthetic trolley. In good weather a doctor on a neighbouring island flew in to assist with minor operations, so at least the equipment she needed was available. Ewan looked down at the array of implements. 'You're going to have to talk me through this,' he told Beth. 'As well as operate. . .'

'I know.' Beth was calmer now. Ewan's humour had lifted the fog of panic and she now knew how she would cope. 'We'll use a relaxant anaesthetic,' she told him. 'In some cases that's enough on its own to make the bowel slide back into place. It happens as soon as the muscles relax.'

'But if it's been strangulating for hours. . .'

'It's unlikely that it will fix itself,' Beth agreed grimly. 'I know. But I can hope.'

'If you want relaxant anaesthetic you'll need to intubate. . .'

'Yes.' Beth thought through the procedure. 'It'd be better if I give the initial anaesthetic and intubate and then you take over while I cut.'

'Much better,' Ewan agreed promptly and drew another smile from Beth. It might work. For all his flippancy Ewan was coolly watchful. As Beth moved to scrub, he started to check through the anaesthetic trolley with Enid. His incisive questions told Beth that she had someone who knew exactly his level of competence and would not go beyond it. The thought was comforting. She had tried to use the previous vet as an anaesthetist in an emergency and had come close to disaster. The man had assumed he was much more knowledgeable than a mere female doctor and had refused to follow instructions.

She took a last look round and nodded. 'We're as ready as we'll ever be,' she said, her voice sounding surer than she felt. 'Bring him in.'

They moved swiftly. Graeme was drowsy with the pre-op medication. 'I'm feeling OK,' he muttered drowsily. 'Pain's gone. Just let me sleep.'

'We'll do that,' Ewan grinned down at him. 'That's why I'm here. To make sure you have a good, long sleep.' He nodded at Beth and Beth swiftly administered enough anaesthetic to relax him completely.

As Graeme drifted into deep unconsciousness and she inserted the tube to breathe him, she swiftly outlined the procedure to Ewan, only to find there was no need. He moved to take control of the airway. 'I've been involved in taking care of pedigree bloodstock for one of the country's leading stables,' he told her. 'If you think we're taking good care of human patients, you should see the medical technology that goes into this country's favourite animals.' His eyes were fixed on Graeme's face, flicking upwards every couple of seconds to the monitor and Beth felt herself relaxing. He knew what he was doing.

Now it was up to her. The hernia site was exposed and Beth looked down, hoping for a miracle. Sometimes they came. If the relaxant anaesthetic let the bowel slip back into position then Graeme could wait for a few days and go to Melbourne for the operation.

There was no such luck today. The bowel stayed protruding, and Beth was forced to continue. She looked up at Ewan and he gave her a faint, encouraging nod. Go on, the look said. I know you can do it.

If only it didn't need resection. . . Beth took a deep breath and cut, exposing the loop of angry purple bowel. She bit her lip as she saw its colour. Was she too late?

Carefully, she extended the gap through which the loop of bowel protruded, easing the pressure. She looked up to Coral, a demand on her lips, but Coral had anticipated her need. The nurse had warm saline packs ready, and Beth carefully positioned the bowel against them. Now. . With the pressure off, all she could do was wait and see whether the bowel was still viable. And hope. . .

The seconds ticked endlessly by. At the head of the table Ewan's eyes went from the patient's face to the monitor and back again in a steady, unceasing vigil. Whatever Beth was doing, his job was to keep Graeme breathing. Intubated — his breathing totally controlled by the tube Ewan was carefully tending — Graeme's life depended much more on Ewan's skill at this particular moment than Beth. A moment's inattention on Ewan's part and the breathing would cease.

The bowel was still purple. Both nurses were silent,

watching eagle-eyed. The waiting went on and on. It's not going to turn, Beth thought hopelessly. She started going through the procedure for resection in her mind, knowing the complications likely to ensue from having an unskilled surgeon do such an operation. Resection needed a competent general surgeon in a major hospital — not a single GP and a vet!

'It's fading,' Enid said softly.

'I don't think so.' Beth kept staring, her mind wanting to believe that the angry purple colour had faded but her eyes not daring to accept.

'Yes,' Enid said definitely, and Coral nodded in quiet satisfaction. These two women were in their element. The quiet hospital was not enough for them to display their many skills.

For it was fading. Suddenly there was no doubt. While they watched, the section of strangulated bowel slowly — slowly — faded from deep purple to light and then, finally, to its normal healthy pink. Beth felt the breath rush from her body in a sigh of relief and wondered vaguely how long she had been holding it. It seemed like it had been for half an hour or more.

'Rats,' Ewan said conversationally, and Beth's eyes flew up to him. He was still looking at the monitor but the grim look on his face had lessened.

'I beg your pardon?' she said blankly.

'I was just starting to fancy myself as an anaesthetist, too,' he smiled, his gaze back on Graeme's face. 'Now I suppose you'll just sew him up and tell me to take myself back to my veterinary practice.'

'With bells on,' Beth smiled, moving to do just that.

Carefully, she pushed the bowel back into the abdomen and stitched the area where it had bulged. She worked swiftly, her heart light with relief. Maybe I should go back to a city hospital, she told herself. I'd never get myself in this awful situation again and. . . She bit her lip. And I could be away from Ewan. . .

So then what would happen to the emergencies on the island? she asked herself savagely. If she left she knew the chances of Illilawa getting another doctor were remote. The island had depended solely on its nurses before she came, and it would do so again. And if something like this happened — well, Graeme Edgar would be dead.

She started the external stitching and glanced up to Ewan. 'Ease up now,' she told him. 'I'll be finished before he comes round and I don't want him under longer than necessary.'

Ewan nodded and his fingers moved to reduce the flow. Moments later they were done. Graeme stirred, his breathing was once again his own responsibility. They waited, the two nurses cleaning up silently behind them, as consciousness gradually returned.

'All over,' Beth said gently as his eyelids flickered open. 'You're minus one bump and a whole heap of pain.'

Graeme managed a weak smile of relief and then closed his eyes again.

'Take him back to the ward,' Beth told the nurses. 'I'll clean up and go and see Mrs Edgar.' She moved across to the sink and Ewan followed.

'Thank you,' she said, her voice containing a faint tremor of uncertainty. Ewan turned on the taps for her and then pulled her around so he could untie the tapes at the back of her gown. 'We. . .we would have been in a mess without you.'

'What would you have done if I hadn't been here?'

Beth shook her head. It didn't bear thinking of. She looked up as the door opened and Enid appeared. 'If we've had enough trauma I might go back to the party,' she told them. 'I've left my husband there.' She smiled dubiously at Beth. 'I gave Dr Thomas a lift,' she explained. She turned to Ewan. 'Will you come back, too?'

'There's nothing else for you to do,' Beth told Ewan. She didn't want him to be so close. Not now. . .

'You mean I'm dismissed?'

'Something like that.' She shook her head and suddenly tears welled up behind her eyes. 'I wish you would.'

'And you?'

Beth shook her head. 'I'll stay here until Graeme's obs settle. But you have to go back. People will be upset.'

Enid looked from one to the other, her bright eyes seeing too much. 'I'll help Coral out here for a moment,' she volunteered. 'Give me a call when you're ready, Dr Thomas.' She whisked herself out of the door again.

'Beth. . .'

'Please,' Beth faltered. 'Please, Ewan. Just go.'

Silence. He stood looking down at Beth's bowed head while the silence stretched on and on. From the other room came the sound of the two nurses softly talking, and the clock on the wall ticked endlessly.

'Please, Ewan.'

His mouth twisted in a wry grimace and his hands came out and caught hers. 'I think I'll have to,' he said grimly.

'It's your party. . .'

'I don't mean the party.' He put a hand up to where a trace of blood ran across her face. Reaching over he found a moist paper towel and wiped the stain away. 'Beth, I mean the island. I can't stay here. . .'

'I knew you wouldn't,' Beth said drearily. The touch of his hand on her face was a physical pain. She tried to smile but it didn't quite work. 'I thought. . . I thought you might stay more than a week, though.'

'Hell!' The expletive broke from him and he pushed her away, turning so he was facing out of the small window to the blackness of the storm-tossed sea beyond. 'Do you think I want to leave?'

'I don't know what you want,' Beth said hopelessly. She spread her hands. She had no pride at all where this man was concerned. 'I only know that you can't cut yourself off from people for ever. I hoped you'd find the courage to stay. I hoped. . . I hoped you'd want me.'

He didn't move. The words echoed around and around the tiny room. They shouldn't have been said, Beth thought bleakly. She was mad.

'Beth, I do want you,' Ewan said. His voice wasn't that of a lover, though. It was the voice of a man driven beyond what he could endure. 'But I'm not. . . I can't marry. . . You must see that.'

'I'm not asking you to marry me.' Beth hardly knew she had said the words. 'I wouldn't. . .'

'I know.' He turned then and came to her. For a moment Beth thought he would grasp her, but he stopped, his body tight with tension. 'You wouldn't ask. You ask nothing, Beth.' He shook his head. 'It's true that when I came to this island I came to get away from people, and now. . .now I'm leaving for the same reason. I have a book to write. I thought here I could do some veterinary work while I wrote, but it seems I can't without. . .without becoming involved again. Beth, I've seen the worst—the worst way that humans can treat each other and it made me not want to be a part of it. I haven't anything to give any more.'

'I'm not asking you to give. . .'

'No. You're not.' He stood there, silent and immobile and Beth thought her heart would burst. She wanted to reach out and touch him but something in his stance stopped her. He was a rock, as cold and as impenetrable as the granite of the island. 'Beth, you ask nothing. It would be easier if you did. . . You give and you give and you give. You even give yourself. . .'

'Ewan. . .'

'Why?' The question exploded. 'Why, Beth?'

Beth took a deep breath and stared straight down at the floor. 'Ewan, I love you,' she whispered.

He stood, silent. For a moment she thought he hadn't heard and pain welled up in her like a raw and aching wound. 'I love you,' she whispered again.

'No.' It was a flat denial. Ewan's voice contained rejection and anger. 'You don't. . .'

'How do you know that?'

'Because there isn't such a thing.' He shook his head as if trying to rid himself of some unwanted burden. 'God knows, Beth, you're old enough to see the world as it really is. How old are you? Twenty-six? Twenty-seven? Too old to be as innocent as you seem.'

'I'm not innocent,' Beth told him, her voice faltering. 'It's just. . . It's just I've never been in love before. . .'

'People don't love. Not really. . .'

'You didn't love your daughter?' The words were out before Beth could catch them and they struck Ewan like a blow. He flinched, and when he looked up at her his eyes were suddenly distant. He was no longer seeing her, Beth knew, but a child toddling towards a pool of sunlit water. . .

'Beth, Sophie was a child. As you are a child. Innocence ends. . .'

'You mean you don't think I can keep loving you? You don't think people can be trusted?'

'No,' he said flatly.

'You don't think. . .' Beth searched for courage. She

held out her hands as if pleading. 'You don't think you can take a chance on this. . .on this feeling. . .'

'Oh, God, Beth. . .' He groaned and his hands suddenly came up to grasp her. He looked down at her and her eyes met his. She was pleading with everything she knew. This was her man. It seemed so right. . .

'No,' he said again, but his hands still held her. He pulled her hard against him and the curves of her body moulded to him. This was her place. 'No. God knows I want you. I want you so much. You are the most beautiful. . .the most precious and desirable of women. . . And if you can find happiness then you deserve it.'

'I'm happy with you.'

'You don't know what you're saying.' He pushed her away then, brutally, cruelly and Beth stood motionless. She was losing. She knew she was losing.

'It's true that I loved Sophie,' Ewan said roughly. 'And what I feel for you. . .' He shook his head. 'It'll end,' he said simply. 'As did Sophie. And I'm not going to inflict that on myself.'

'By leaving, isn't that what you're doing?'

'If it has to be,' he said harshly, 'then it might as well be now.' He turned and walked out of the door.

'I wish it could be now.'

Beth said the words over and over again as she lay and stared sleeplessly into the dark. Her bed seemed cold and hard. She was over-tired but sleep was impossible. 'And it's going to be impossible while Ewan Thomas is still on the island,' she said sadly to herself. She went over and over what had been said that night, her whole body burning at what she had done.

'I love him and he doesn't want me,' she whispered. 'And now he's leaving.'

When? Beth lay listening to the waves crashing onto the beach. This weather could go on for days. Ewan couldn't leave yet. And even when the weather cleared. . .'He'll have to give notice. It could be weeks before he leaves,' she whispered into the dark. 'How can I face him again. . .?'

CHAPTER ELEVEN

BETH walked into the clinic the next morning as Enid returned to take over from Coral. The two nurses were deep in conversation as Beth entered the foyer. They broke off as Beth arrived and she managed a smile for both of them. When the clinic was empty the two nurses had days to themselves but they had been working every second shift for over a week.

'Are you two gossiping?' she asked weakly.

Coral blushed bright crimson and Beth cringed. Stupid of her to ask, she thought bitterly. She knew what they'd been gossiping about. So as well as Ewan going the island would know that he'd taken her heart with him. The knife twisted deeper.

'How. . .how are our patients?' she managed. 'What are Graeme's obs doing?' Somehow she managed to get the conversation back to normal but the nurses' eyes still held the touch of sympathy. Beth ignored it. It was the only way she could cope — to pretend everything was normal.

'They're all well.' Coral hesitated. She picked up her handbag from the desk as a prelude to taking herself home. 'Well. . .' she said slowly, as though reconsidering. 'Mrs Bource telephoned her parents early this morning, asking them to organise her transport to the mainland separately from her husband. She says what he does is no longer any of her business.'

Beth nodded. After last night she had expected no less. She thought back to the night of the wreck, though, and felt a flicker of doubt. There was good within John

Bource. He had clung to his young son with the desperation only a real father could show. Why was he failing to show that devotion now?'

'He's just a big kid,' Coral said sadly, guessing Beth's thoughts. 'He's afraid to grow up.'

Graeme Edgar was groggy but recovering. He greeted Beth with a smile.

'Thanks, Doc,' he said weakly. 'It was so good to wake up without that pain.'

'You would have saved us a lot of worry if you'd come and seen me earlier,' Beth growled. 'Or told me when we were helping you with the calf.'

He nodded wearily. 'Next time I will,' he promised. 'Only there isn't going to be a next time.'

Beth smiled and left him sleeping. At least there was one source of satisfaction this morning. She walked from the room and almost collided with Ewan as he strode through the door.

'Beth. . .' The word was broken off as if he caught himself in some illicit act. His hands came up and then fell again. 'How's our patient this morning? I came to check.'

'Fine,' Beth said stiffly. 'I. . .' She swallowed and tried again. 'Excuse me, please. I'm busy. . .'

'Beth, I'm tendering my resignation to the island committee this morning,' he told her brusquely. 'I'll be leaving as soon as possible.'

'Fine,' she managed.

'Beth, for God's sake. . .'

'Damn you, Ewan Thomas,' she whispered.

The door back to Graeme's ward closed behind her and they were left alone in the foyer. To her horror, Beth felt her control slipping. 'Damn you. I was happy here. Happy! And then you came with your smile and your laughing eyes and your. . .' She broke off, fighting for logic to what she was trying to say. 'For once in my life you made me feel I'm someone besides somebody's daughter and somebody's doctor — and then you tell me that you don't care. That you can't love. That you'll hurt me if you stay. Well, you've already hurt me, Ewan Thomas. I know, it's not fair to feel the way I do. You didn't ask me to feel like this but you've hurt me worse than I've ever been hurt in my life. You tell me it's a mistake to love because it just causes pain. Maybe you've just proved yourself right!'

'Beth. . .'

'Get lost,' she whispered hopelessly. 'You can't leave this island fast enough for me, Ewan Thomas. And just. . .just go!'

'Doc! Doc Thomas!' The yell pierced the glass door and somehow also managed to pierce Beth's rising misery. She caught herself, choking back a sob, and looked up to see Fergus Mackervaney striding fast across the hospital entrance.

'Doc Thomas!' Fergus pushed back the big glass door and then stood, fighting to get his breath back.

'What is it, Fergus?' Ewan cast a doubtful look at Beth and then concentrated on the elderly farmer. 'What's the problem?'

'I've just driven up from the farm along the west coast-road,' Fergus said. 'There's a bunch of pilot whales beached beyond Jefferson's Point.'

'Pilot whales. . .'

'Six of them as far as I can see, though there might be more by now,' the farmer said miserably. 'There were four — three adults and a calf and then two more came ashore while I watched. Just drove themselves up on the sand as though they were intent on suicide. There were more whales out to sea but I reckon I frightened 'em off. I hauled a hub-cab off the car and stood up to my waist in the surf, thumping the metal with a stick beneath the water until they disappeared out to sea again. But there are six well and truly stranded, Doc Thomas, and they'll die for sure if we can't get 'em back in the water.'

Beth stared in horror at the elderly farmer's sodden clothes. 'Fergus Mackervaney, you're soaked to the skin and it's freezing! You'll give yourself pneumonia.'

'Don't fuss about me, girl,' Fergus told her. 'It's them whales I'm worried about.'

Beth looked at him in dismay. Most of the islanders felt the same way about the pods of pilot whales sighted periodically off the coast of Illilawa. They were held to bring luck to the island. The fishermen held strongly to the belief that when the whales were close the fishing was better. For whatever reason, their coming was always welcomed with pleasure.

'Six,' she said slowly.

'One calf and five mature adults,' Fergus said morosely. 'And they're big 'uns.'

'Oh, Fergus. . .'

'They die a miserable death left stranded on the beach,' Ewan said slowly. He shook his head. 'Pilot whales. . . There's no way we'll refloat them. I'll organise a couple of helpers and we'll go out and put them down.'

Both Fergus and Beth regarded Ewan as if the man had taken leave of his senses.

'Put them down?' Fergus demanded. 'Don't be daft! As vet for the island I thought you'd co-ordinate the rescue.'

'Rescue. . .' Ewan looked at them blankly. 'Do either of you have any idea of what's involved in refloating whales? It's a massive effort. Pilot whales need at least ten adults to move one, and they have to be refloated simultaneously or they rebeach. Are you expecting the three of us to just go down there and pull them out to sea?'

'Of course we're not,' Fergus said drily. 'I know how big they are.'

'And how carefully they have to be treated,' Ewan went on. 'It'd take close on every man on this island to move them.'

'Plus the women and kids,' Fergus agreed.

Ewan stared. 'It's freezing out there,' he said. 'No one's going to help us get the whales off the beach. . .'

'Who says?' Fergus demanded belligerently and Beth shook her head. She looked up at Ewan and saw blatant disbelief in his eyes. This man expected good of no one. Well, maybe he'd be surprised. The island honoured the whales, and took pride in the creatures using the sea around Illilawa for their breeding grounds.

'Try us,' she said gently.

No more whales had grounded themselves by the time they reached the beach. Beth and Ewan drove separate cars around to Jefferson's Point so that Beth could return if she was needed. Fergus stayed behind to find some dry clothes and to alert the islanders.

Even though no more whales had beached themselves the ones that had were in deadly trouble. They lay wallowing in the shallows, their massive forms writhing in a useless effort to free themselves of the sand. They looked huge even from the road as Beth pulled her car to a halt. By the time she emerged from the car Ewan was already standing on the headland and gazing bleakly down at the mighty creatures.

'What a waste,' he said bitterly. 'What a damnable waste!'

Beth shook her head. 'Not yet,' she whispered. She walked swiftly down the beach, ignoring Ewan. She was dressed for a morning in the clinic, in skirt, sweater and sensible shoes and the wind cut around her legs like a knife. She ignored the discomfort, her mind intent on the plight of these lovely mammals.

At the water's edge she stopped and stood still, her mind racing. Beth had been involved in a whale rescue once before, but it had been that of a smaller pygmy sperm whale. Ewan had said it would take ten people to move one of these creatures and he was right, though maybe he was underestimating. While she watched, a whale near her lifted its tail and lashed uselessly downwards. A massive spray rose, soaking Beth to the skin. She shuddered, but the shudder wasn't just from the cold.

Ewan came silently up behind her. At their feet was the calf. Even it was huge. It would take six strong men to move it, Beth thought.

'Why on earth do they do this?' she asked. She shook her head. 'It seems so pointless.'

'I can guess.'

Beth looked wonderingly up at the man beside her. He was staring down at the calf. Bending down, he ran a finger across the animal's jaw. When he rose he showed the finger to Beth. 'Sump oil,' he said wearily.

'You mean they're ill?'

'Not necessarily.' Ewan wiped his finger across his cord trousers as if ridding himself of something disgusting. 'It only takes one. If the calf ingested oil and became ill and disorientated it may well have beached itself. Its distress cries will have brought the others in. It's just as well Fergus came when he did. The whole pod can follow and thirty or forty whales have been known to beach themselves at any one time.'

'Oh, Ewan. . .' Beth looked down at the calf. Knowing what she was looking for she could clearly see the oil around its jaw. 'It must have swum into a mass of the oil. . .'

'I've brought what I need to euthanase them,' Ewan said, his voice as bleak as Beth felt. 'It's going to take some doing, though, while they're as active as they are.'

'We'll try to refloat them,' Beth said flatly. 'We'll use euthanasia as a last resort.'

'Beth, it's impossible.' Ewan shook his head, his gaze going from one creature to the next. 'Six whales. That's sixty people at the very least, plus back-up. These people would be in the water for hours. The whales will have to be refloated and then rocked in the shallows while they get their balance. It's freezing. On a popular city beach on a summer's day I'd say we had a chance, but not here. . .'

'Why not here?'

'Because people don't care,' Ewan said flatly. 'On a hot day in holiday season it's a trendy thing to do — to save the whales. Here. . . Here would take real commitment. . . This would involve discomfort — even pain. I can't demand that the islanders do this?'

'You mean no one will help because there's nothing in it for them?' Beth said curiously. 'You really do think the worst of people, don't you?'

'Yes,' Ewan said flatly.

'If we get the volunteers, will you help?' Beth's voice was curiously detached. Half of her was still aching with love for this man beside her, but the other half was disengaging itself completely from what he was saying. She couldn't think that he was right.

'How are you going to get the volunteers?' Ewan said jeeringly. 'Offer them payment from the non-existent hospital funds?'

'They won't have to be paid,' Beth said quietly. She looked back along the headland in the direction of the settlement. 'And I don't think you need to ask how we're going to get the volunteers. They're already on their way.'

Ewan stared. Along the coast road was a straggly line of every conceivable type of vehicle, all heading in their direction. Beth counted back. Twenty. . . Twenty-five. . . She looked in the other direction and smiled. The island's telephones had been humming. There were trucks coming down from the opposite direction, and from inland. Volunteers. . . People who cared. . .

Matt Hannah was one of the first to arrive. He swung himself out of his truck and jogged down the beach, his florid face intent. 'Well,' he said. 'Only six! I was afraid there'd be more.'

'Only six,' Ewan said slowly, his eyes riveted to the people disgorging themselves from the vehicles up on the road.

'Shouldn't be too much of a problem,' Matt said. 'We had a beaching a few years back and lost most of 'em but we didn't have a vet then. Just tell us what to do, Doc.'

Ewan shook his head. 'I can't let you people risk your lives — hell, Matt! That water's straight from the Antarctic!'

'We know that,' Matt said scornfully. 'I've Betty at the telephone exchange ringing round to find every wetsuit on the island. All the fishermen here have waders, and most of the farmers too, come to think of it. Every person here knows how to look out for himself in bad weather.' He grinned at Ewan. 'I even threw in a spare pair of waders and another sweater into the truck for you, Doc, cause you came out here in such a hurry I knew you'd forget 'em.' He frowned at Beth. 'And you can get off the beach until you're properly geared too, Dr Beth. You know the dangers as well as us.'

Beth grinned. 'Yes, sir,' she said happily. She looked up at Ewan and smiled at the look of stupefaction on his face. 'I'll go back to the clinic, change and come back when I can. Restrict time in the water, Matt, regardless of wetsuits, and get a fire going on the beach. A big one. I don't want anyone suffering from hypothermia.'

'The wife's bringing a heap of dry wood in the other truck,' Matt told her. 'Come back as soon as you can, girl. A bit of immediate medical treatment might be handy.'

Beth looked at Ewan again. 'So you reckon you can refloat?' she said.

'Of course we can,' Matt said definitely. 'I'll have every able-bodied man, woman and child down on the beach in less than half an hour. We should be able to do the thing.' He too looked up at Ewan, his face for the first time reflecting a trace of uncertainty. 'Isn't that right, Doc?'

Ewan shook his head as though ridding himself of a bad dream. He looked across at the whales. 'I don't know what condition they're in,' he said slowly. 'The calf's ingested oil — though it looks pretty active. . .'

'But we can give it a try,' Matt said. His face reflected distress and Beth knew that darn near every islander would be feeling the same.

Ewan looked again at the mass of people coming down the embankment. More were arriving every minute. He looked across at the whales and took a deep breath. 'OK,' he muttered. He looked up. He had made his decision and his face showed it.

'Matt, in the back of my truck there's a spool of blue plastic ribbon,' he said, his voice firming at every word. 'I want numbered ribbon attached to the tail of every animal, with care taken while we do it. A blow by the tail could knock a person unconscious. Once they're tagged I'll examine each of them in turn. I want all the whales to be moved to an upright position with their heads facing seawards, moving them only by the bulk of their main trunk. We'll need five people or more on each side of every animal to hold them until they settle in the right position. The most important thing is to get the blowhole free from sand and above water. Do we have a megaphone?'

'You bet we do,' Matt told him.

'OK, let's move.' Ewan was already striding across the beach. 'We need to register every helper on the beach, so we can assess how long they're in the water. I want no useless heroics.' He turned back fleetingly to Beth. 'And get off the beach, Dr Sanderson. I don't want anybody here who's not dressed to help.'

'No, sir.' Beth smiled, the pain around her heart easing. She saluted and left.

Beth had a surgery booked at nine but when she arrived there was no one there. She walked through to the hospital to find Enid on duty. 'Everyone's on the beach,' the nurse told her. 'You think they'll worry about coughs and colds when they could be splashing about in freezing water rescuing whales?' She shook her head. 'Mad, I call it.'

'Are you saying you wouldn't be on the beach if you weren't on duty?' Beth smiled and Enid laughed and shook her head.

'I'd be there,' she said. 'The school's closed because the teacher reckoned the kids could be useful. Every able-bodied person on the island must be there.'

Beth nodded and then frowned as John Bsource walked into the clinic. The man was wearing a perpetual scowl.

'I came to see my wife,' he said sullenly.

'I'm sorry.' Beth sighed, not liking what she was going to have to do. She moved to stand between John and the entrance to the ward. 'Your wife has said that she doesn't want to see you, and last night your yelling disturbed the other patients.'

'I didn't yell.'

'You were drunk,' she said harshly. 'And you yelled. Mr Bource, do you know what's going on with the whales?' Beth asked, trying to deflect the man's rising fury.

'The whole damned island is out trying to save a few fish,' he said belligerently. 'I had to make my own breakfast at the guest-house.'

'Do you know why they've beached themselves?'

'I wouldn't have a clue.' Behind them the door opened silently and Robyn Bource appeared. 'It's no business of mine.'

'One of the whales hit a patch of your oil,' Beth continued. 'It got disorientated and ended up on the beach, and the rest of the whales followed it in.'

'So you blame me. . .'

'Us,' Robyn said in distress. 'Oh, John. . .'

'Look, it's hardly our fault,' John Bource said, turning to his wife. 'We weren't to know. . .'

'The whole island's out undoing our damage,' Robyn said tremulously. 'John, you have to help.'

'I'll give a cheque. . .'

'No.' Robyn took a deep breath. 'John, money's not enough any more. You have to help.' She stared at him. 'If you want any more to do with me and your son then you have to help.'

'Robyn. . .'

'I mean it, John,' she said softly. She looked down at the baby. 'I can't. Not with Sam. But you can and you should.'

'But it's bloody freezing. . .'

'I know,' Robyn said wearily and turned to go back into the ward. 'And I don't care. You still should.'

John Bource stared after her. He took a step forward but Beth was still blocking his path. Finally, he held up his hands and glared at Beth and Enid. 'Women,' he said, and slammed out of the clinic.

Enid shook her head. 'Just a kid,' she said slowly. 'I don't know that Robyn and Sam have a chance.' She looked at Beth. 'Are you going back to the beach?'

'I'd better.' Beth brought her mind sharply back from the Bources' problems. 'I'll get changed, organise some gear and get down there. Regardless of precautions, there'll be problems working on the beach in this weather.'

It was the beginning of a very long day. The islanders worked in shifts. Ewan organised them in teams of sixteen people per whale, keeping the animals moist, their blowholes clear and periodically rocking their massive bodies while they prepared them for return to the water. As the tide went out and the animals were left high on the beach, those not rocking the whales formed chains to cart buckets of water up to the carers. Others were digging channels from the whales back down to the shore, so that eventually the whales could slide back into deeper water.

Beth took her vehicle down on to the beach near the fire, opened the big back doors and termed it a medical station. She was busy from the time she arrived.

'We'll have to wait until high tide to try and move them,' Ewan told her, 'and I'll need people in the water until then.' He had come over to ask Beth to check each volunteer as they changed shifts. Like Beth, he was concerned about hypothermia going unnoticed, and his concern kept his discussion with Beth brief and impersonal. 'Full tide's at six tonight. We'll move them all back into the water then.'

'Will they live that long?'

'They're all in good condition,' Ewan told her. 'Apart from the calf.' He looked doubtfully at the smaller animal. 'It's weaker than the others. We'll try.'

'I don't think these people will accept failure,' Beth said softly. She looked around the beach. There were scores of people in the water. The teams who had just been relieved were warming themselves by the fire. On the grass verge leading up the road the women had set up huge trestle tables bearing hot soup and sandwiches. 'Enough volunteers for you, Ewan?'

He cast her a strange look. 'Just about.'

'And what are you paying?' she couldn't resist saying, and then paused in shock. John Bource was walking down from the road, his expression half belligerent and half shamefaced. He was obviously unsure of his reception. 'I don't believe what I'm seeing,' she murmured.

Bource approached them hesitantly. His look was defiant and yet oddly hesitant. 'I. . .' He shook his head. 'Give me a job,' he told Ewan.

Ewan nodded non-comittally. 'There's a wetsuit in the pile near the fire,' he said. 'Choose one that fits, and then join the team caring for the calf.'

'The calf. . .'

'The smallest whale,' Ewan explained patiently. 'It's in a bad way.'

'Is that the one that hit the oil?' Bource's voice sounded sullen and Ewan sighed.

'We think so,' he said. He turned his back on the man as someone called him from the other side of the beach. John Bource stared across at the beach for a long moment and then went to follow instructions.

Beth stayed all day. She wore her beeper, but there was no call back to the hospital and Beth was needed where she was. She moved among the volunteers, quietly checking and ordering people home to rest when she saw they were doing too much. Most went for an hour, warmed themselves and then reappeared.

John Bource surprised everyone. He had obviously decided that if he was going to help, then he was going to put in an all-out effort, and his fight to save the calf became personal. He stayed in the water long after his shift and had to be ordered out by Beth.

'You'll make yourself ill,' she told him, and he looked down at the floundering calf and gave a wry grimace.

'Yeah,' he said. 'That'd be poetic justice.'

Finally the waves came creeping back again with the tide. As the water level rose, Ewan organised tarpaulins on ropes. The whales were inched onto the canvas as the water raised their huge bodies.

'We'll take them out into shoulder-deep water,' Ewan told the assembled workers. 'They'll need to be rocked in the water for half an hour or more before we release them, so they can regain their stability. We release them all together. Otherwise they'll just rebeach.'

He walked over to the calf and stood, looking down. Beth hesitated and then went over to where he stood.

'You don't think this one will make it?' she said.

Ewan shook his head. 'I doubt it.' He stared down. 'I'd like to put down a tube and rehydrate, only the damned thing is so big. If it writhed halfway through I could end up puncturing the stomach.'

'So we just wait and see. . .'

'That's the trouble,' he told her. 'If we do. . . If it's in trouble back in the water it might well bring the adults in again. We might be better putting it down now.'

'No.' John Bource looked up from where he was carefully ladling water over the whale's back. 'No!'

'John, if we must. . .' Beth started.

'No,' the man said again fiercely. 'I'll haul it out to sea myself if I have to.'

'I thought you said they were just fish,' Beth reminded him. Bource was pale and strained, as if near to some invisible breaking point.

'Yeah, well. . .' He stared down. 'There's still oil in its mouth. My oil. . .'

'Your oil,' Ewan agreed. He hesitated. 'All right. We'll give it a chance in the water. If it gets its balance, then we take a punt and hope to hell it makes it.'

Beth flashed a look up to Ewan. This wasn't the sensible choice. To risk the pod for the chance to save a calf. . . They could rebeach. . .

'We'll just have to refloat them if they rebeach,' Ewan told her, reading her thoughts. 'Because the calf deserves a chance.'

It was a massive effort to get the animals back floating and what followed was the hardest time of all. Volunteers stood shoulder-deep in the rough water, rocking the whales from side to side, waiting for them to adjust to the sea again. Left at this point they would have simply sunk to the bottom and drowned.

For the watchers on the beach it seemed even harder. To watch and wait. . .

Half an hour went by and Ewan moved from team to team in the water, checking each whale. As he emerged from the waves Beth went down to meet him.

'They're all buoyant,' he said briefly. 'Apart from the calf.'

Beth stared up at him. The people around them fell silent too, waiting for his verdict.

'We give it another fifteen minutes,' he said. 'I'm

risking problems if I have volunteers in the water longer than that.' Only the strongest swimmers were out in the water now and they were having trouble keeping their feet in the strong swell.

'And after that. . .'

'Then we pull the calf out and put it down,' Ewan said harshly. 'It's the only way.'

Beth knew he was right, but the next fifteen minutes were the longest she had known. Finally she could bear it no longer. She slipped up the beach and donned a wetsuit, telling herself she had to check the volunteers in the water.

The people on the beach stood silent. They had worked so hard. Now they were forced to stand idle — waiting. Beth waded out, checking on each group around the whales. She left the calf until last.

It was still in trouble. Ewan was at its head. John Bource and the team were strongly supporting it, but as she approached, Beth saw it was still wallowing off balance. She looked away from the creature, forcing herself to concentrate on the volunteers. They all seemed to be coping, with the exception of John Bource. He was white-faced and weary. Each wave was flinging him off his feet and Beth knew he was at the last stages of exhaustion.

'It's time to come out, John,' she said gently.

John looked at Ewan and his mouth set in a grim line. 'You'll kill it, won't you?'

Ewan shook his head. 'If it dies it won't be me who has killed it.'

'What's that supposed to mean?'

'I don't have to tell you, Bource.'

The man's white face tightened further and if Ewan had been within striking range Beth knew he would have lashed out. Another wave caught him and he fell.

Beth caught him as he emerged, spluttering, from the foam.

'John, you've done all you can. . .'

'But it'll die!' The man was past reason. Whatever control he had was gone. His voice rose into a hopeless groan. 'It's true. I killed it!'

'No.' Ewan's voice cut across John's. 'No. Look!'

Within the grip of the team who held it, the whale's body tightened and flexed. The unbalanced sway ceased, and the whale righted to a swimming position. 'Wait,' Ewan said softly. 'Wait.'

They did. Beth hardly knew she was breathing. They waited and watched, and all around them the teams holding the adult whales also waited. Five minutes. Ten. Every moment Beth could see the little whale recovering more. Fifteen. . .

Fifteen! How long could these people stay in the water? She looked around at the team. Without exception their faces were blue-white from the cold. They could wait no longer. She moved across to Ewan but he was before her.

'We go now,' he said softly. 'We can't wait longer. I want every able person in the water making as much noise as possible. If we could swim with them then we would, but in these conditions it's impossible. I want the whales to know that they have to head out to sea.'

Out to sea. . . Out to sea the rest of the pod would be waiting. If the whales could get out past the cove. . .

The teams spread the word. Beth should go back to the beach. She should. . . She stayed right where she was, watching and waiting, the freezing water surging around her shoulders. Then Ewan raised his hand. Simultaneously the teams fell behind their whales and motioned them forward.

For a long, long moment the whales stayed immobile.

If they were disorientated—if they turned and headed
back into the cove—then there was nothing the people
here could do to prevent them rebeaching. 'They
mustn't,' Beth whispered, her words lost in the din the
volunteers were making. They mustn't. . .

Then slowly—slowly—as if unsure of the welcome
waiting for them in the open water—the whales started
forward. One of the animals turned slightly sideways
and for a moment Beth thought it would swing around.
Its swimming slowed and it stopped.

No, she screamed, but no word sound came out. You
can't stop now. No. Then the calf came up beside the
huge creature and Beth realised what had happened.
The mother was waiting for her child. The calf came up
beside it, the bigger creature turned her eyes to the
open sea, and they were gone.

Beth was crying. She stood, sobbing helplessly at the
sight of their massive bodies moving away. Close by her,
she was aware of John Bource doing the same. Then a
hand gripped hers under the water. She turned and saw
Ewan. His eyes were a blaze of triumph—tenderness
and joy. 'We did it,' he told her. He grabbed her and
swung her up over the waves and then caught her to him
as she came down. 'We did it, Beth Sanderson. We did
it!'

She was laughing and crying all at the same instant.
Dimly, she was aware of being kissed and her hands
tightened on the man holding her. Her heart was with
the whales, swimming strongly further and further from
the dangerous shore.

CHAPTER TWELVE

By the time the beach had been cleared it was after nine. Everyone was tired and hungry but no one wanted to go tamely home to bed.

Beth was kept busy until the end. There were a couple of volunteers suffering hypothermia, including John Bource. 'You should head straight to bed,' she told him. He nodded.

'In a while.' He seemed dazed and unsure — a man with the stuffing knocked out of him — and Beth's eyes followed him in concern.

'You're coming back to the pub?' Matt Hannah asked her, as John stumbled up the beach to where the local school bus was waiting to transport volunteers back to the settlement. 'The hotel's putting on a free feed!'

'In a while.' Beth's gaze went over to where Ewan sat before the fire. He was writing notes while the information was still fresh in his mind. All the data obtained tonight would be recorded at a central registry with Project Jonah, to be used for future beachings.

'We've done a damned fine job,' Matt told her, following her gaze. 'We're lucky that young fella's here.'

'He's leaving,' Beth said softly. 'He won't stay.'

'Leaving?' Matt shook his head. 'Don't be daft, girl. He's only just arrived.'

Beth would have preferred to go quietly to bed, but she was not permitted. She managed a few private moments to shower and change, and then Micky Edgar arrived,

Buster peering importantly from the neck of his sweater.

'Mr Hannah said you're wanted at the pub,' he said. 'It's compulsory.'

Beth smiled wearily. Sometimes she would like to live some place where she could go home and lock the door. 'I'll be over soon, Micky,' she promised.

'Buster and I kind of thought you'd drive us,' Micky said hopefully. 'Mum brought me here but she's staying at the hospital. The pub's a really long way and. . .and Buster's tired.'

'Micky,' Beth began and then sighed and stopped. Why bother fighting it?

The whole island seemed to be in the pub. Beth stopped at the door, unsure how to break through such a mass of people, but Matt was watching out for her. He called her over and it wasn't until Beth approached his table that she saw a seat had been reserved for her beside Ewan. She cast a confused look at him and then sat down, her cheeks burning. Ewan was deep in conversation with one of the local fishermen. He looked up at her as she sat, his eyes creasing into a wry smile, and then he turned back to his conversation.

Somehow Beth got through the night. The talk swirled around her in a noisy, indecipherable jumble. People laughed and sang and congratulated themselves and Beth was happy for them, but she couldn't be happy for herself. Not while Ewan was sitting there. . .

Ewan too was silent, listening to the laughter and talk but contributing little. He was watching her. Beth could feel his eyes on her and it made her worse. How long before she could politely leave?

'Dr Beth?'

It was a man's voice coming from behind her. Beth looked around to see John Bource making his way through the crowded room. At his side was his wife, and in his arms was his baby son. 'Dr Beth?' he said anxiously, as if unsure that she would even acknowledge him.

'Yes?' Beth looked at Robyn and then looked again. Robyn Bource's expression could only be described as radiant.

'We wanted to tell you that I'm moving over to the guest-house tonight,' Robyn told her, smiling happily. 'I. . . We thought it was time.'

'Robyn means I've come to my senses,' John Bource said, holding his wife tightly to him and speaking loudly to be heard above the din. 'Can we. . .can we talk to you outside a moment?'

'Sure.' Beth was glad to escape the stifling heat and noise of the hotel. She rose, aware of Ewan's eyes still on her.

The silence outside was almost eerie after the din within. The Bources stood on the veranda overlooking the sea while John Bource struggled to find words. Finally, he took a deep breath and spread his hands.

'Beth, I've been a damned fool,' he said awkwardly. 'Since Sam was born — well — it seemed that all of a sudden gates were slamming shut. I had to be responsible. Robyn and I couldn't have fun any more.' He shook his head. 'I nearly killed them, and I still couldn't see. And then tonight — ' he paused, as though trying to find a way to go on ' — tonight I saw what that damned oil did — and then the whale calf swam out to sea and its mother stopped and waited — well, it made me see just how right the whole thing was. Parenthood, I mean. Responsibility and all the trappings. And how much I wanted to be a part of it.'

'I'm glad,' Beth smiled. 'I'm very glad for both of you.'

'Regardless of the weather, we'll stay on for a week or so,' he continued. He looked down at his baby son. 'We. . . I have to get to know my son, and this is a great place to do it. We wanted to tell you of our decision, though, and to thank you for your help.'

'It was my pleasure.'

'I know,' John Bource said. 'The lady of the generous heart. Robyn and I wanted to do something though, just to show you how much we appreciate your help.' He turned to Robyn and smiled. 'It's your gift, honey. You say.'

Robyn smiled happily back and looked down at Beth. 'We've decided to make a gift of two oxygen concentrators to the island. One so Lorna can go home, and one to act as a spare in case someone else needs it.' She gripped her husband's hand. 'We're together, and now Lorna and Fergus can be together, too.'

Beth gazed at the pair in astonishment. 'Do you have any idea what they cost?'

'Yes,' John told her. 'Enid and Coral gave us details. We can afford it.' He grinned. 'So far we've had more money than sense. If we get rid of some money maybe we'll develop some sense.'

'That's just wonderful.' Beth gave Robyn a swift hug and then leaned over the baby to give his father a kiss. 'It's just wonderful. . .'

They left her then. Beth stood on the veranda, staring out to sea. The cheerful laughter from the hotel beckoned her back inside, but she didn't return. She took a step forward from the veranda and then stopped. Ewan materialised from the shadows and stood, blocking her path.

'Going home, Dr Sanderson?'

'Yes,' she whispered and didn't move.

'I'll walk with you.'

'I. . . I have my car.'

'So do I,' Ewan smiled. 'Maybe they can escort each other home.'

'Ewan. . .'

'Beth.' He smiled down at her and it was the smile she had believed he possessed. The belief wasn't based on certainty. She hadn't seen it. This smile — well, a pale shadow of it aimed at Micky had made her heart turn over and now — now it was directed at her and it made her want to weep. He held his hand out and took hers in a strong clasp. Pulling her away from the light of the hotel he led her down towards the beach.

'It's a long way home around the beach,' Beth managed.

'Good,' he said, and smiled again. There was nothing left for Beth to do but follow.

They didn't speak until the hotel was left far behind them. There seemed a thousand things to say but no words to say them. Beth's mind was whirling with questions but she could get no further than the feel of Ewan's hand holding hers. For now. . . For now all she could do was wonder.

The wind had died and the beach was cold but calm. The moon was hidden by a haze of low-lying cloud but a silver sheen showed through. Beth was warmly dressed in jeans and sweater. She should be warm, she thought as she walked across the damp sand. So why was she trembling?

Ewan felt it. He stopped, swearing softly. Pulling his leather jacket from his shoulders he put it around her.

'I don't want it,' Beth said faintly. She gave a half-hearted tug on her hand. 'Ewan, I don't want to walk home.' She tried to pull the jacket away from her shoulders. 'Please. I don't want anything from you.'

She didn't look at him. She couldn't. Beth's eyes

focused on a piece of Ewan's thick sweater. She daren't look up.

It seemed she was forced to. Ewan's hand came up and cupped her chin, forcing her eyes up to meet his. 'You demand nothing, do you, my lovely Beth?'

'I'm not. . .'

'You ask for nothing and you trust everybody. And somehow it works miracles. John Bource. . .'

'You heard?'

'I heard. The Beth Sanderson gift. To make miracles happen.'

'I don't,' Beth said shakily. 'Ewan, please. . . Let me go.'

'No.' His hands came around to grip her waist and he held hard. It was as if he was making a vow.

She looked wonderingly up at him and he smiled. 'No,' he said again, and she wondered at the sound of his voice. He sounded young. And he sounded free. The prison bars were lifting.

'Beth, I went back to the party last night determined to leave this damned island,' he said softly into her hair. 'And a young lady who was suffering from rather too much to drink told me how dull it was here. "No shops," she said. "No restaurants. No cinemas. Nothing!" She told me I'd be crazy to stay.' His grip tightened. 'Beth, do you find it dull?'

Beth shook her head. Her face was brushing the coarse wool of Ewan's sweater. 'No,' she whispered. 'I guess not. Just. . . Just lonely.'

'Well, that's something we don't have in common,' Ewan said seriously. 'I agreed with her that there were things in the city I couldn't find here. But I don't miss them, Beth, and I never will. Because the one thing of any value at all in my life is right here. The one person who fills my heart. . .who can make me smile. . .'

'Ewan. . .'

'Beth, Celia soured my view of the world. It stayed sour until I saw what one caring heart can achieve. And then, this morning, I stood on the beach and I saw the world caring again. And I thought. . .' He laughed then, a joyous, carefree laugh, full of promise of the things to come. 'I thought it was a great place to be. For the first time since I lost Sophie I thought it was OK to be a part of the human race again. And I thought. . .' He sighed and moved his lips into her hair. 'I thought of you. All day I've been thinking of you. I've been treating those damned whales and I've been wondering how long it would take to get them afloat so I could get you alone and tell you. . .'

'Tell me what?' Beth's words were a whisper on the night air. Her heart was singing inside her.

'Tell you that your miracle has worked. Tell you that you've given me love and in turn I give it back to you. Tell you that I want you, Beth Sanderson — I want you more than I have ever wanted a woman in my life before. I want to marry you. I want to live with you for the rest of my life, and I want us to have children together. Because it's still a wonderful world, my Beth. You've given me that. Somehow you've given me back my gift of loving.'

Beth said nothing. She couldn't. Her voice wasn't working any more. The cold of the beach was forgotten. Joy was running through them like a current, back and forth, intermingling in their entwined bodies.

'Do you want to hear a plan?' Ewan asked gently, his face in her hair, and Beth didn't have to nod to acquiesce.

'A plan?'

'While you were showering and changing I went to

see Fergus Mackervaney. I've been thinking for a while and tonight Fergus agreed.'

'To what?'

'He's sold me his farm,' Ewan told her. 'He'll act as manager and stay in the house with Lorna as long as he's able. We'll build on the other side of the property.' He smiled down at her. 'The original plan was for the sale to give them enough money for the oxygen concentrator, but it's still workable. This means that they'll live comfortably for the rest of their lives with no money problems and we can have a share in a farm. As well as a medical and veterinary practice.'

'Oh, Ewan. . .' Beth felt her heart would burst. To live here forever. With Ewan. . .

'It's dependent, though, Beth,' he said seriously. His hands held her to him in fierce possession. 'It depends. . .'

'On what?' She could hardly whisper.

'On whether one green girl will agree to be my wife. Will you marry me, my lovely Beth? You share your love but I want more. I want to share your life.'

She looked up at him then and her heart dissolved in a mist of gentle joy. Ewan was smiling down at her and his eyes held a trace of uncertainty. Or fear? It was as if he was unsure. . .

How could he be unsure? How could he not know how much she loved him.

'Ewan,' she whispered and the one word held all her answers. She put her hands up to touch his face but before she could, he had pulled her up to meet him. His lips met hers, touching, tasting, claiming her as his own and he was hers.

'Ewan,' she whispered again but it was her heart that whispered. She struggled to make her lips say the words. The words that would seal her happiness for always. . .

'Of course, my love,' she managed. She raised her lips to be kissed again and around her the waves crashed in a crescendo of sheer joy. 'It's not my life any more. It's ours.'

Full of Eastern Passion...

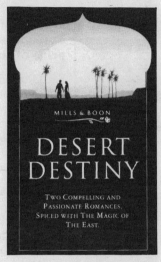

Savour the romance of the East this summer with
our two full-length compelling Romances,
wrapped together in one exciting volume.

AVAILABLE FROM 29 JULY 1994   PRICED £3.99

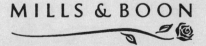

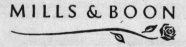

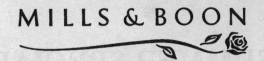

MILLS & BOON

LOVE ON CALL

The books for enjoyment this month are:

HEARTS OUT OF TIME Judith Ansell
THE DOCTOR'S DAUGHTER Margaret Barker
MIDNIGHT SUN Rebecca Lang
ONE CARING HEART Marion Lennox

♥ ♥ ♥ ♥ ♥

Treats in store!

Watch next month for the following absorbing stories:

ROLE PLAY Caroline Anderson
CONFLICTING LOYALTIES Lilian Darcy
ONGOING CARE Mary Hawkins
A DEDICATED VET Carol Wood

LOVE ON CALL
4 FREE BOOKS AND 2 FREE GIFTS
F R O M   M I L L S   &   B O O N

Capture all the drama and emotion of a hectic medical world when you accept 4 Love on Call romances PLUS a cuddly teddy bear and a mystery gift - absolutely FREE and without obligation. And, if you choose, go on to enjoy 4 exciting Love on Call romances every month for only £1.80 each! Be sure to return the coupon below today to: Mills & Boon Reader Service, FREEPOST, PO Box 236, Croydon, Surrey CR9 9EL.

— — — — — | **NO STAMP REQUIRED** | — — — — — —

YES! Please rush me 4 FREE Love on Call books and 2 FREE gifts! Please also reserve me a Reader Service subscription, which means I can look forward to receiving 4 brand new Love on Call books for only £7.20 every month, postage and packing FREE. If I choose not to subscribe, I shall write to you within 10 days and still keep my FREE books and gifts. I may cancel or suspend my subscription at any time. I am over 18 years. Please write in BLOCK CAPITALS.

Ms/Mrs/Miss/Mr _____   **EP63D**

Address _____

_____

Postcode _____ Signature _____